A Deadly Promise

A Deadly Promise

❖ ❖ ❖

Joan Lowery Nixon

BANTAM BOOKS
NEW YORK • TORONTO • LONDON • SYDNEY • AUCKLAND

A DEADLY PROMISE

A Bantam Book / February 1992

The Starfire logo is a registered trademark of Bantam Books, a division of Bantam Doubleday Dell Publishing Group, Inc. Registered in U.S. Patent and Trademark Office and elsewhere.

Library of Congress Cataloging-in-Publication Data

Nixon, Joan Lowery.
A deadly promise / Joan Lowery Nixon.
p.   cm.
Summary: Sarah risks her life to clear her murdered father's name and expose big time criminal activity in the lawless mining town of Leadville. Sequel to "High Trail to Danger."
ISBN 0-553-08054-7
[1. Mystery and detective stories.   2. West (U.S.)—Fiction.]
I. Title.
PZ7.N65Db   1992
[Fic]—dc20   91-22184
                                                                                    CIP
                                                                                    AC

Published simultaneously in the United States and Canada

PRINTED IN THE UNITED STATES OF AMERICA

BVG   0   9   8   7   6   5   4   3   2   1

Chapter 1

◆　　◆　　◆

Sarah Lindley waited impatiently for her younger sister, Susannah, to arrive on the Leadville stagecoach. Unwilling to leave the large front window of the Grand Hotel, she blew on her hands, stamped her feet to keep warm, and tried to keep her mind off the heavy snowfall outside. She had overheard someone saying that dangerous weather on the trail had caused a serious stagecoach accident on Mosquito Pass. Fortunately, the Spotswood and McClelland coach on which Susannah was traveling would be coming through Weston Pass. Clint Barnes would be driving, and this meant that Susannah was in good hands.

Sarah had prepared everything for Susannah's arrival except what and how much she would tell her sister. It had been at Susannah's insistence, after their mother's illness and death, that Sarah had come to Leadville in search of their father, determined to bring him home to Chicago. It had been a terrible shock to discover that Ben Lindley was a fugitive, accused of murder. Sarah had found him in his mountain hideaway and had shared only a few moments with

1

him before he was shot and killed by a vengeful gunman who had followed Sarah to her father.

For just an instant Sarah would have given everything to be back home in Chicago with Susannah and Mother. If only Mother hadn't died and mean, greedy Uncle Amos and Aunt Cora hadn't moved in and taken possession of the boardinghouse! Why did everything have to change? Why couldn't it remain the same?

Tears burned Sarah's eyes, and she brushed them away with the back of one hand. It was impossible to go back. After Father's burial she had sent Susannah a telegram and traveling money she had borrowed from one of Leadville's most successful bankers, Homer Morton, instructing her to leave Chicago and come to Leadville; and she had applied for a teaching position in one of Leadville's elementary schools. Sarah had reservations about asking fifteen-year-old Susannah to come to this wild mining town, but she had given her promise to Father. She would clear his name by bringing to justice the thieves he had tried to tell her about as he died in her arms. Somehow, she must fulfill his last request.

It wasn't going to be easy. She had no idea who Father had meant when he had spoken of the greatest robberies in Leadville being committed by a few people who were more vicious than the footpads and lot jumpers. Who were these people? And what and where was the proof Father had hidden? How in the world would she begin to find it?

It began to grow dark, and as Sarah watched a lamplighter light the lamps on Chestnut Street, one by one, she thought again about what she'd tell Susannah. All that Susannah knew was the contents of the telegram—that Father had died and she must come to Leadville as soon as possible.

Susannah had obeyed without question, but Sarah knew her sister would have many questions when she arrived. Sarah planned to tell Susannah that Father had been a gambler. And she'd tell her about Eli Wulfe. But what about Father's whispered secrets and Sarah's promise to him? So far, Sarah was the only person in the world who carried the burden of that knowledge.

At last, with a rumble of wheels, the big Concord stagecoach pulled up in front of the hotel. Sarah eagerly watched Clint vault from the driver's seat to open the door of the coach.

An elderly woman stepped from the coach, followed by a young woman and two men, but no Susannah. After two more men descended, Clint swung the door shut. Surely Susannah wouldn't have missed the stagecoach! What had happened to her?

The lone young woman turned toward the hotel. The moment she spotted Sarah standing in the window, her face glowed with excitement. "Sarah!"

Clint, who had picked up the last satchel—undoubtedly Susannah's—stopped and turned toward the window, too, and his expression as he saw Sarah was every bit as bright and eager as Susannah's.

Clint loves me, Sarah realized. Clint Barnes, whom she'd met when he had driven her stage to Leadville, was a hardworking man with a goal: a ranch of his own, a wife with whom to share it, and children. He wanted Sarah to be his wife, and Clint was not a patient man. Although he hadn't yet spoken of love, Sarah could look into his deep blue eyes and see the intensity of his feelings.

Calm down. Take one step at a time, Sarah reminded herself.

As Clint and Susannah hurried into the lobby Sarah ran

3

to meet them, and she clung to her sister, murmuring, "Susannah, Susannah."

Finally, Sarah held Susannah at arm's length and studied her, amazed at the change in her younger sister. Susannah's waist was tightly corseted, accentuating the roundness of her hips and bosom; and with her light brown hair piled high in a twist under her bonnet, Susannah was pretty—*very* pretty. "I was looking for a child," Sarah said. "At first, I was afraid you hadn't come."

"How could I have traveled as a child, in short skirts with braids down my back?" Susannah answered. "I would have been sent right back to Uncle Amos, and goodness knows it was hard enough to find the chance to break away." She held out her hands. "I put my hair up and my skirts down, and see, I became a woman."

Sarah laughed and gave Susannah another hug. "That change is supposed to take place on the day you're sixteen, and you only became fifteen a few weeks ago."

"No matter," Susannah said. "I packed some of Mother's clothes. Most of them needed just a small amount of taking in, and now they fit me perfectly. I want nothing more to do with those childish, loose cotton dresses and horrible, long black stockings I used to wear."

Clint stepped up and put a hand on Sarah's shoulder, giving it a gentle squeeze. Sarah rested her own hand on top of his, glad—so very glad—that he was there.

"Susannah was a good traveler," he said. "Not a word of complaint the whole way."

"Clint took good care of me," Susannah murmured. She tilted her head, looked up at Clint from under her lashes, and smiled.

If she hadn't known better, Sarah would have thought

4

Susannah was flirting with Clint. She put an arm around her sister's shoulders. "It's getting late," she said. "Let's go home."

"Home?"

Sarah hurried to say, "Our Leadville home. You'll like Mrs. Hannigan, our landlady. She's friendly and kind and eager to meet you. Her boardinghouse is much like ours, and you and I have a large corner bedroom to share."

Clint picked up Susannah's satchel, and the three of them headed out the door into the din and crowd of Chestnut Street. Sarah heard a shot and cringed. How could a town continue to exist when it remained so lawless?

Twice she'd been accosted since she'd begun teaching nearly four weeks ago, so she carried money only if she was going shopping. There had been more talk about the organization of the Merchant's Protective Patrol, but so far the members had done nothing to protect the citizens. What could they do against all the criminals who had come to Leadville for easy money?

It seemed to Sarah that Susannah hadn't heard the gunshot. Maybe she didn't even recognize the sound. She stared at the crowded tangle of pedestrians, horses, and wagons and asked, "What's happening here? Where are all these people going?"

"It's like this night and day," Sarah said. "The saloons and gambling houses stay open, and—" she broke off. "Watch out for that drop in the sidewalk. You'll soon learn to keep your eyes on the ground as you walk, so you won't fall."

A carriage pulled in front of a wagon, and Jeremy Caulfield shouted, "Sarah! I tried to come sooner, but Uncle was using the rig. Climb in! Hurry!"

5

Although Clint's eyebrows dipped into a frown and he muttered something under his breath, Sarah was thankful to see Jeremy's carriage. The walk to Mrs. Hannigan's would have been miserably cold.

Jeremy was dressed in a high-buttoned, heavy wool suit— the perfect picture of a serious-minded reporter. Sarah had met Jeremy on her trip from Chicago to Leadville, and she knew from traveling with him that he was not serious-minded. He was as full of fun and mischief as Sarah's father had once been. With Jeremy, every day would be an adventure; and if an adventure didn't come along, he would go in search of it. He was thoughtful and kind . . . and *very* nice to look at, Sarah admitted to herself.

After quick introductions, Jeremy helped Sarah into the carriage and took her cold hands in his, rubbing them briskly. His smile was so eager that Sarah thought with wonder, *He loves me, too.*

Although she was not far from her eighteenth birthday and was being courted by two equally wonderful men, Sarah couldn't allow herself to fall in love until she had completed the task her father had given her.

As the four of them rode through the traffic it was hard to talk over the shouts of the pedestrians and the blasts of music coming from many of the buildings, but Sarah saw Susannah take careful note of the carriage and the matched pair of horses, then give a silent nod of approval.

Sarah was eager for Susannah to meet Jeremy's uncle, Chester Caulfield. He'd been kind to let them use his carriage. Ever since they'd met he'd been thoughtful and friendly to Sarah, taking an active interest in her search for her father. During the weeks since Father's death, Mr. Caulfield and his wife had often invited Sarah over. Jeremy had

6

already invited Sarah and Susannah for dinner on Sunday evening, and Sarah knew the Caulfields would be every bit as friendly and gracious to Susannah as they had been to her.

As Susannah leaned close to talk to Clint in the back-seat of the carriage, Jeremy bent his head to say to Sarah, "Today I interviewed a man named Dan Dougherty who has come here from Independence, Missouri. He's been telling people that Jesse and Frank James are quietly working a claim near Soda Springs."

"If that's true," Sarah said in surprise, "then Jesse James couldn't have been the one who robbed our train."

"It's true, all right," Jeremy answered. "Mr. Dougherty recognized Jesse and talked with him when he saw him in Charlie Lowe's saloon. He said that Jesse asked about his mother with tears in his eyes."

Sarah well remembered the outlaw's eyes staring at her over the bandanna that masked his face as he robbed their train. "Have a drink on Jesse James!" he'd called, tossing a silver dollar to the conductor. But if they weren't Jesse James's eyes, whose eyes were they? They may have belonged to some robber who hoped to make use of Jesse James's fame, but it was more likely someone who wanted Jesse James to take the blame.

"Who do you think the robber was?" Sarah asked Jeremy.

He shrugged. "Could have been one of the Daltons or the Younger Brothers. Maybe Doc Holliday, Bat Masterson, or even Harley Emmett, who's considered the worst of the lot."

He pulled the carriage to a stop in front of Mrs. Hanni-gan's, climbed out, and tied the horses' reins to the hitching post, while Clint helped Sarah and Susannah from the carriage.

7

Inside the warmth of Mrs. Hannigan's parlor, Susannah was introduced to each of the boarders. Mrs. Hannigan, her cheeks red with pleasure, gave Susannah a hug.

"What a dear girl you are," she said as she looked from Susannah to Sarah and back again. "Most people might not see a family resemblance, but I do, even though Sarah must have favored her father, and Susannah looks the perfect image of her mother."

Susannah turned to Sarah with surprise, and Sarah explained. "Father left a photograph of Mother. I keep it on the table next to my bed."

"I know you must be hungry." Mrs. Hannigan shooed Susannah, Sarah, Clint, and Jeremy toward the kitchen. "Clint Barnes," she said, "there's no telling when you last ate. I made stew and lots of it, knowing you were coming. There's plenty for all."

As they ate and talked, Sarah couldn't look away from her sister—her dear, wonderful, loving little sister. Susannah had always been like Mother in her manner and attitude, but now with her womanly hairdo and clothing, Susannah was practically Mother's double, and Sarah was mesmerized.

Susannah told one anecdote after another about her travels to Leadville until her words dissolved in a yawn.

Sarah pushed back her chair and stood. "It's time for bed," she said. Taking her sister's hand, she helped her to her feet.

Clint's eyes were on Sarah. "We were the last coach to make it through the pass because of the heavy snow," he told her, "so I'll be having a few days off."

"Good," Mrs. Hannigan interjected. "That means you can come to the dance and box supper on Saturday evening at the Clarendon Hotel. It's to raise funds for the Harrison Hook and Ladder Company."

Confused, Susannah looked to Sarah. Sarah smiled and explained, remembering the evening she had first heard of box suppers.

She had been in the kitchen with Mrs. Hannigan and Jeremy, warming herself by the stove after a cold walk home from the schoolhouse.

"Do you know how to dance, Sarah?" Jeremy had suddenly asked. Without waiting for her answer, he put one hand at Sarah's waist and began to twirl her around the kitchen, counting, "One two three, one two three."

Although Sarah never had attended a dance, she had easily followed Jeremy, her long, full skirt and petticoats sailing out around her. As the impromptu waltz ended, Sarah had leaned against the kitchen table and laughed with pleasure.

"The members of the Harrison Hook and Ladder Company are hosting a dance and box supper fund-raiser on Saturday evening at the Miners Hall," Mrs. Hannigan said. "There'll be a good turnout for it among the decent, hardworking folks in Leadville."

Jeremy made an exaggerated bow before Sarah. "May I request the pleasure of your company at the dance?"

"Only if you'll escort Susannah, too," Sarah had said. She hugged her shoulders, grinning at Jeremy. "I've missed Susannah so much. I don't know how I can wait until tomorrow."

Jeremy's smile faltered for only a second. "I'll consider myself doubly fortunate to be able to escort both the Lindley sisters."

Mrs. Hannigan rattled on as though she were talking to

9

herself. "I'll fill up the boxes with something especially good. The men always like roast chicken and biscuits. And I've got some dried apples stored away to make a good pie. Or should I bake a gold cake?"

"Dinner in a box?" Sarah asked, suddenly aware of what Mrs. Hannigan was talking about.

Mrs. Hannigan's eyes widened in surprise. "Haven't you been to any box suppers, Sarah? Each woman brings a box— some of them tied with ribbon and some fixed up real fancy—and the men bid on them. The winner gets the box of good food and the woman who brought it as his supper partner."

"You can show me your box, Sarah," Jeremy said, "so I'll know it in advance and can bid on it."

"Now, you know that's not fair," Mrs. Hannigan scolded. "Of course, there is always a certain amount of sly whispering going on about which box belongs to which lady, but the donors of the boxes are supposed to be unknown."

"Do the men bid money for the boxes?" Sarah asked.

"Oh, my, yes!" Mrs. Hannigan said. "You should see the amounts that change hands! Some of those men get so carried away that they even toss in gold dust and nuggets, just to get the boxes they want."

"The *supper partners* they want," Jeremy added and winked at Sarah.

Grabbing her hand, Jeremy interrupted Sarah's daydream. "I'll be picking up Sarah, Susannah, and Mrs. Hannigan," he said to Clint. "The carriage holds only four, or I'd offer you a ride."

"We'll meet you there," Sarah said to Clint.

Clint looked down at his heavy boots. "I'm not much for dancing."

10

He was so handsome, Sarah thought, with his black, curly hair and his eyes that were so blue, so deeply, marvelously blue. "I'm not either," Sarah told him, "but Mrs. Hannigan says it will be a wonderful evening. Please come, Clint."

His glance darted in Jeremy's direction. "All right. I'll be there," Clint said.

As he tugged on his heavy, sheepskin jacket, cap, and gloves, Clint moved close to Sarah and said in a low voice, "Susannah was curious, but I left the telling of what happened to your father up to you." He reddened a little as he offered, "If you'd like me to be with you when you talk to her, you can count on me."

"Thank you, Clint. You're very kind," Sarah said. She rested a hand on his arm. "But I think she'd want me to speak with her privately."

He nodded. "Just remember. I'm here if you need me."

"Thank you," she said again. "I'll remember."

At the door Jeremy stepped aside and quietly asked Sarah, "Why don't I stay while you talk to Susannah? It's going to be difficult for you both, and perhaps I can help."

"Dear Jeremy," Sarah said, and in a rush of affection she took one of his gloved hands between her own. "Thank you for offering, but this is something I'll have to do alone."

Chapter 2

◆　◆　◆

Upstairs in the bedroom they would share, Sarah placed the oil lamp on the chest of drawers and said to Susannah, "I'll help you unpack."

But Susannah had picked up the photograph of their mother and was studying it. "I do look like Mother when she was young," she murmured, and Sarah could hear the wonder and pleasure in her voice. "This could be a photograph of me."

When Susannah's things had been hung in the wardrobe and placed in the top dresser drawer, she and Sarah undressed. Susannah heaved a sigh of relief after removing her tight corset.

"You don't have to wear that, you know," Sarah said, but Susannah shook her head.

"I am not going back to being a child. I no longer have a child's body." She quickly pulled her heavy flannel nightgown over her head.

Sarah smiled. When Susannah was determined it was useless to challenge her. Sarah buttoned her nightgown up to the neck and took the pins out of her hair, letting it fall down her back.

"You have such beautiful hair," Susannah said with a sigh. "I wish my hair were a glorious deep red, like yours."

"Yours is lovely and just right for you," Sarah said. She took the amber hairpins out of her sister's hair and picked up a brush. "Sit down here," she told her, pointing to the small lady's chair that stood near the bed. "I'll brush your hair for you."

She moved the brush in rhythmic, even strokes. It was soothing, and she hoped Susannah would relax and want to sleep. "You must be very tired," Sarah said to her sister.

Susannah reached up and took the hairbrush from Sarah's hand. "I'm tired, but before I go to sleep, I want to hear exactly what happened to Father, and why you sent for me. I came against my better judgment, because there is no telling what Uncle Amos and Aunt Cora will do to our property while we're away." Her brush strokes became furious as she spoke of her mother's brother and his wife, who had taken over the boardinghouse as though it were their own. She broke off, and her voice softened. "Even though you haven't given me a good reason why, Sarah, I came to Leadville because you're my sister and I trust you."

"Sit with me on the bed," Sarah said. She held Susannah's hand and began telling her sister everything about her search for their father.

"You actually conversed with a painted woman?" Susannah interrupted. "One who worked in a saloon? Sarah!"

"The woman, Lily, had information about Father." Sarah went on to explain how she had found out about their father's real occupation.

"Our father was a gambler?"

14

"Yes. He played cards for money at both the Texas House and Owens' Faro Club."

"What's faro?"

Sarah shook her head, impatient to get back to the telling. "Faro is some kind of gambling game, but that isn't important," she said. "Listen. There's more I have to tell you."

When Sarah explained about going to the Texas House in her search for Ben, Susannah cried, "You actually went inside a place like that? Sarah! What would Mother have said?"

Sarah was well aware of the tight-lipped disapproval Mother would have shown, although it was more disappointment than disapproval she'd usually seen in her mother's eyes—disappointment that Sarah was dreamy and imprudent like her father and not practical-minded and efficient like Susannah. *You were wrong about me, Mother,* Sarah thought. *And maybe you were wrong about Father, too.*

"Susannah, ways in the West are very different from ways in a civilized city like Chicago," Sarah said firmly, and found herself mimicking something Jeremy had told her when they first met on the train leaving Chicago. "My job was to find Father, not concern myself with rules of etiquette."

She told Susannah what the waitress, Bessie, had said about seeing Father shoot Ezekiel Wulfe at the Texas House only after Wulfe had drawn his gun first. "Lily knew that Father was innocent, too, but then she was murdered," Sarah said. "And soon afterward Bessie disappeared."

It was difficult to continue, but Sarah briefly told Susannah about Father's close friend, Emma Fitch, whose house was ransacked before she was murdered.

Sarah held out her arms and enfolded her sister as she

15

talked about discovering Father's hideout, and they cried together as she explained how Eli Wulfe had burst into the cabin to avenge his brother's death.

Against her will Sarah pictured Eli Wulfe as he stood at the entrance of the shack at Emma Fitch's mine. Eli was a tall, large-boned man, filling the doorway with his presence and his hatred.

"Oh, Sarah." Susannah sobbed and hugged Sarah tightly. "He could have shot you, too."

"I had a gun," Sarah said quietly. "I tried to keep Eli from shooting Father, but I only wounded him."

Sarah would never forget how desperately she had tried to protect her father. She had drawn the small Colt derringer Clint had given her—the one she swore she could never use. She had shot Eli, but she had not been able to keep him from fatally wounding her father. Then she had held her father in her arms—the father she had not seen for ten years—as he died.

Susannah sat upright and stared at Sarah through red, swollen eyes. For just an instant her mouth hung open. A tear trickled down the side of her nose as she said, "You've changed, Sarah. I can see it in the way you talk and move. And now you tell me you shot a man."

"Only to try to save Father. Look at me. I'm still Sarah. You've grown a little older, and I have, too. And I love you even more than I ever did before." Sarah held Susannah's head against her shoulder and smoothed back the hair from her forehead.

Susannah's tears finally ebbed, and she got up to find a handkerchief. She mopped at her eyes and blew her nose, then turned to face Sarah. For a few moments she studied

Sarah's face, then said, "I think you had better tell me all of it."

"A-all?" Sarah was caught off guard. She should have known Susannah would guess if she held anything back, but she still wasn't sure she knew how much she wanted to tell.

"Yes, all," Susannah said. She handed a clean handkerchief to Sarah and sat back on the bed. "The logical thing for you to have done after Father was buried would have been to come home to Chicago. Since you didn't, and since you wanted me to come to Leadville to be with you, there must have been a strong reason."

Susannah paused and pursed her lips as she thought. "It might be Clint or Jeremy. I've seen the way they look at you."

Sarah sighed. She had intended to protect Susannah from the danger there might be in knowing the rest of their father's story. "I promised Father I would do something for him," she said, keeping her voice low.

"Have you done it? What was it? Do you want me to help?"

"Good gracious!" Sarah said, and held her hands up to stop the tide. "I'll tell you. Give me time."

Carefully, as well as she could remember, she told Susannah what their father had said about discovering a crime that was taking place and how he should have gone to the authorities—to Pinkerton's. "He said he had proof and had hidden it where the criminals would never find it. Father thought it would ensure his safety," Sarah explained. "Then Eli Wulfe burst into the room, and . . ."

It hurt so to remember, but she went on. "Father's last words were, 'Remember . . . your mother . . . Margaret . . .' "

When Sarah had finished, Susannah sat quietly for a few

17

minutes. Then she said, "His last words were, 'Remember Mother.' That's odd. Of course you'd remember her."

"I haven't been able to understand it, either," Sarah said.

"What have you learned so far?"

"Not much. I had to take a job teaching school in order to support us and to help repay the money the bank lent me to pay your way here."

"Have you found out anything at all?"

"I learned that Pinkerton's is a national private detective agency."

"Why would Father want you to tell something to Pinkerton's?"

"Perhaps he didn't trust the local officials. I've asked questions, and I've listened to conversations. For instance, you'll find that Mr. Vonachek always seems to know more about what's going on in Leadville than any of the local newspapers. According to him there's been talk in town about some of the members of the police force being in league with some of the lot jumpers—the men who steal other people's property in town—and a few people have their suspicions about Marshal Kelly's honesty."

Susannah interrupted. "Mr. Vonachek is the nice-looking tall man with the blond mustache who came into the kitchen, isn't he?"

"Yes." Sarah was surprised.

"How old do you think he is? Twenty-eight? Thirty?"

"Thirty-two, I think Mrs. Hannigan said." Sarah laughed, wondering why Susannah would care.

"He's seems like a real gentleman; don't you think so?"

"I suppose so," Sarah said, although she hadn't thought about it until then.

Susannah returned to their former topic of conversation.

18

"Think about what Father said—that the greatest robberies in Leadville were being committed by a few people who were stealing in a hidden, more vicious way."

"Yes. Those were his exact words."

"Was he talking about murderers? Maybe gangs, like the Jesse James gang?"

"I don't think so," Sarah told her. "The gangs never seem to try to hide their crimes."

"Father told you he had proof, giving the names of these people and what they did. That sounds like a document of some sort—maybe a list. He must have hidden it somewhere he felt was safe. Do you have any idea where that might be?"

"I thought it might be with Mrs. Fitch," Sarah answered. "When I found her—her body—the house and everything in it had been torn apart. Wallpaper had even been ripped from the walls. If the people responsible for her murder were the ones Father knew about, then they must know about the existence of this proof, and that's what they'd been searching for."

"And probably found."

"On the contrary. I think the fact that *everything* in the house was torn and destroyed means there's a strong possibility that they *hadn't* been able to find what they wanted. They didn't stop looking until they had wrecked the whole house."

"That's very clever of you, Sarah," Susannah said. "I think you must be right."

"Also, Mr. and Mrs. Fitch were Father's closest friends. I'm sure he'd have realized that anyone who held this proof would be in danger. He wouldn't have put them in jeopardy."

"Yes, but even if Mrs. Fitch didn't have possession of Father's proof, whoever killed her thought she had." Susannah suddenly shivered and rubbed her eyes. "I'm too tired to think about this any longer, Sarah, and I'm getting colder. Let's go to bed."

Sarah snuffed out the wick in the oil lamp, and they climbed under the layers of heavy quilts. Sarah had no sooner settled herself than Susannah asked, "Sarah . . . tell me about Father. What was he like?"

The memory of the way Ben Lindley had looked—gaunt and haggard and filthy—brought Sarah to the verge of tears again. She gulped them back and tried to make her voice warm and reassuring. "Father was tall and strong and handsome," she lied, "with that wonderful sparkle in his eyes."

"Did he ask about me?"

"Oh, yes! Almost the first words he spoke to me were, 'How is your mother? How is little Susannah?' He loved you so much, and he loved Mother. When I told him Mother had died, he cried as though his heart had broken."

"But he abandoned us."

Sarah grasped her sister's hand. "Who knows why he did? Maybe it wasn't his fault alone."

"Are you saying it might have been partly Mother's?"

"We'll never know what problems grew between our parents, but we can be sure that they both loved us in their own ways."

"You may have forgiven him, Sarah, but I don't know if I can."

"Of course you can. He loved us."

For a few moments Susannah was silent. Then her fingers relaxed, and soon Sarah heard her steady breathing.

Susannah had fallen asleep, but Sarah remained awake

and tense, staring into the blackness of the room as part of their conversation came back to her.

Susannah had been right. It hadn't mattered whether or not Mrs. Fitch had hidden the proof Father had talked about, because whoever had killed her *thought* she had it in her possession. If they hadn't found it, they'd keep looking and keep wondering who else Father could have given it to. And sooner or later it might occur to them that if the proof had been in his possession, he probably would have given it to the person who was with him when he died.

His daughter . . . Sarah.

Chapter 3

◆   ◆   ◆

On Friday morning Susannah accompanied Sarah to school. Susannah had protested, but Sarah insisted, saying, "I can use your help." She couldn't tell her younger sister that she was afraid to let her out of her sight. It stood to reason that if Sarah was in danger, Susannah could be, too.

The children in Sarah's class were immediately curious about Susannah. One teacher was enough to have to please. Were they going to have to get used to *two*?

It was a long and difficult day. First Sarah asked Susannah to listen to the reading lesson, but it did not go well. Mercy, who was every inch as tall as Susannah, took Susannah's presence in the classroom as a challenge and showed off by reading faster and faster until Susannah stopped her and bluntly told her to start over, because no one could understand what she was saying.

Susannah was just as tactless with the youngsters struggling over their multiplication tables, telling them to stop being lazy and to get busy memorizing the tables, or they'd all be headed for the poorhouse.

Finally, about forty minutes before their hour-and-a-half noon break, during which the teachers and children walked home for dinner, Sarah invited Susannah to sit in a chair near the back of the room and enjoy reading Father's book of poems. It was not until it was time to dismiss the students that Sarah glanced at Susannah and saw that the book was on the floor and her sister was impatiently fidgeting in her chair.

On the walk back to Mrs. Hannigan's boardinghouse, Susannah complained, "How can you stand dealing with all those children every day?"

"They're wonderful children," Sarah answered, "and they're eager to learn. You'll soon come to enjoy working with them."

Susannah stopped suddenly, the familiar determined, stubborn look in her eyes. "Sarah," she said, "teaching may be something you like to do, but I do not, and I don't intend to go back to the classroom with you."

"But Susannah . . ." Sarah fell silent. She didn't want to alarm her sister by expressing her fears.

Susannah surprised Sarah by saying, "You've made it clear that you're worried about me, and after our conversation last night, I'm worried about you, but we have to be sensible. I have no intention of spending my days with that dreadful Mercy Klinger, especially when there is something I'd much rather do."

"What is that?" Susannah asked cautiously.

"I'd like to work in Mrs. Hannigan's boardinghouse. It's work I know I'm good at. You worked there for a while, so why can't I?"

Sarah considered the idea. Susannah would be just as safe in Mrs. Hannigan's care—maybe safer than she would be with Sarah. "It's a possibility," she answered. "Of course

24

you'd have to wait until Mrs. Hannigan needs to hire extra help."

"Didn't you notice? Mrs. Hannigan was upset this morning because whoever was supposed to help at breakfast hadn't shown up. Come to think of it, I might be able to prove my worth right now." Susannah began to walk quickly toward the boardinghouse, and Sarah had to trot to keep up.

Mrs. Hannigan chirped with joy and put Susannah to work immediately. After the noon meal Sarah walked back to school alone, her derringer in the purse that swung from her left arm.

When class was dismissed at four that afternoon, Sarah saw Clint waiting outside the classroom and forgot her fears. As he walked her back to the boardinghouse, he asked, "Did everything go well when you talked with Susannah?"

"She was shocked," Sarah told him, "but she took everything in stride."

"She's got spunk," Clint said. He smiled at Sarah approvingly. "And so have you."

"Spunk? If I have, it's something new to me."

"No. It's something you were born with."

She shook her head. "I've always been called a dreamer."

Clint nodded. "There's nothing wrong with that. Everybody has dreams." He paused, flipped back his coat, and rested his hand on the grip of the gun on his hip as two men headed toward them.

The men suddenly turned in the opposite direction, and Clint nodded, continuing what he was saying. "I told you my dream—about the ranch I'm going to own. There's too much that's wrong in a town like this, but using the land as it should be used—well, that's clean and good and will help Colorado to grow the way it should. I'm getting closer to it, Sarah. Come spring, I'll have enough money saved."

"I'm happy for you, Clint," Sarah said.

His sun-browned face crinkled with pleasure. "Now, why don't you tell me your dream?" he asked.

"I had so many dreams when I was younger," Sarah told him. She smiled, dismissing them. "My old dreams were like dandelion puffs that blew away. I don't know yet what I want my new dream to be . . . or if I'll ever be able to make it come true."

"You will. You've got what it takes."

They walked a few moments without talking, while Sarah tried to see herself as Clint had seen her. Did she really have the ability to make a dream come true? Father hadn't been able to, and Mother had often told Sarah that she was like her father. But Sarah had changed since she had left Chicago. She felt it. She'd surprised herself by the decisions she'd made and the things she'd done.

Clint's voice dropped as he asked nonchalantly, "How are you going to decorate the box you're bringing to the box supper?"

Sarah glanced at Clint and laughed mischievously. "You know I'm not supposed to tell you."

"No one's going to know?"

"If you mean Jeremy," she answered, "he won't know either."

Clint smiled. "Maybe I can bribe Susannah to tell me."

They reached Mrs. Hannigan's front door, but before Sarah opened it, Clint said, "I'd like to come calling after supper."

"Oh, Clint," Sarah said, "I'm sorry, but Mr. and Mrs.

26

Caulfield want to meet Susannah, and I promised we'd visit them this evening." She could see the disappointment in Clint's eyes, and she rested a hand on his arm.

"Sarah, come riding with me tomorrow morning," Clint said. "Out there it's peaceful enough so you can hear a clump of snow fall from a branch. We'll go early, even before the chickarees and pine martins are up. There's only a thin layer of snow in the meadows, and we're bound to spot a fox and elk and maybe some bighorn sheep. Have you ever seen the small tracks the deer mice make on the snow?"

"I'd love to go!" she said, then hesitated. "But Susannah's just arrived in Leadville. I shouldn't leave her."

"You want me to ask Susannah to go with us?"

"Yes. No! I forgot—Susannah now has a job working for Mrs. Hannigan, and she'll be busy with breakfast. Maybe I should help her. Maybe . . ."

"You have a job of your own," Clint reminded her. "Let Susannah take care of her own job, and you come with me. Please, Sarah?"

His *please* warmed her down to her toes, and she leaned even closer to him. "What time should I be ready?"

"Six o'clock."

"It will still be dark."

She could feel his warm breath against her cheek. "I can set my mind to wake at any time. If you're not up, I'll wake you." He smiled. "If it's necessary, I'll throw pebbles against your window."

The front door was thrown open. "Oh, there you are, Sarah," Susannah said, but her eyes were on Clint, and she smiled. "Don't stand out here in the cold," she told him. "Come inside."

27

"No, thanks," Clint answered as he backed down the porch steps. "I understand you ladies already have plans for this evening."

"I'll see you tomorrow morning—early," Sarah told Clint, and reluctantly followed Susannah into the house.

As Sarah tugged off her boots, Susannah gave her a quick, sideways glance and asked, "Who do you like best—Clint or Jeremy?"

"They're both very nice," Sarah answered. She felt her cheeks grow warm.

"You know what I mean. They're both courting you."

Sarah sank into one of the parlor chairs, thankful that she and Susannah were alone. "Jeremy's exciting," she said. "He looks for the fun in life, and he makes me laugh. He has dreams. . . ." She stopped, remembering her conversation with Clint. "Of course, Clint does, too. Clint's quiet, but he's kind and caring." She smiled at her sister. "And very handsome."

Susannah gave a little nod. "They're both handsome."

"None of this matters," Sarah told her. "I haven't got the right to make plans for myself until I've done what Father asked me to do."

Susannah sat across from her. "And just when is that going to take place?"

Sarah groaned. "I don't know. I think of Father's words, of every single thing he told me, and I can't imagine where he hid that proof."

Susannah sighed. "Frankly, all this secrecy and mystery are giving me a headache. If Father didn't give you enough information to carry out his wishes, then you can't be bound by any promise you made to him."

"It wasn't his fault," Sarah protested. "He was badly hurt. He was dying, and he found it hard to speak."

"Still, the fact is that Father is dead, so what can be gained now by trying to salvage his reputation?"

"The people he spoke of are still stealing."

"Then it's a matter for the law to take care of, not us," Susannah said dismissively. "You know, Jeremy told Mrs. Hannigan that his father's holdings are substantial, and Jeremy is on an allowance from a trust fund."

When Sarah didn't answer, Susannah went on. "Jeremy's uncle and aunt are childless, and Jeremy stands an excellent chance of being promoted into a good position on the newspaper and perhaps inheriting it one day."

Sarah stared at her sister with surprise. "Exactly what are you trying to say?"

Susannah sighed. "Stop daydreaming, Sarah, and pay attention. You're attracted to Jeremy. I know you are. I'm telling you that you should put that promise to Father out of your mind. It's time for you to begin thinking about your future, and if you keep putting them off too long, you may end up losing both your suitors."

Sarah was shaken. For just an instant she wondered if her promise was partly an excuse to avoid making a choice between these two wonderful but very different young men. She had never before considered the possibility that if she waited too long, she would no longer have any choice left to make.

Chapter 4

• • •

Sarah and Susannah handed their wraps to the Caulfields' maid and entered the ornate living room, which was bright with oil lamps on every table. Sarah had assumed they'd be the only guests, so she was surprised to see the banker, Mr. Homer Morton, and his wife, a plump woman who was introduced as Mrs. Morton.

Mrs. Morton—jewels gleaming against the deep red velvet of her dress—clasped one of Sarah's hands and one of Susannah's. "What rare beauties you have found us," she trilled to Jeremy, but her initial glances seemed appraising, even suspicious.

As usual, Chester Caulfield's timid wife, Violet, fluttered in the shadows like a tiny, silent moth that wished to escape.

After dinner the ladies retired to the living room while the men remained in the dining room to enjoy an after-dinner glass of port wine and a cigar. Mrs. Caulfield settled softly into a corner of one of the large sofas, but Mrs. Morton filled a commanding, plush-upholstered chair and took charge of the conversation.

"I was very sorry to hear about the death of your father," she said. Her glance swept both sisters but settled on Sarah. "I know it must have been difficult for you to discover that your father was . . . well, that he had shot a man."

Shocked at the woman's bluntness, Sarah cried, "He shot in self-defense!"

"Oh?" Mrs. Morton looked surprised. "Not according to the account of the shooting that I read in *The Star*."

Sarah looked helplessly to Mrs. Caulfield. "Mr. Caulfield's newspaper? He wrote *that* about my father?"

Before Mrs. Caulfield could answer, Mrs. Morton said, "My dear, you can't blame a newspaperman. A newspaper must print whatever is news."

"But Father . . ."

Mrs. Morton interrupted. "I heard you were with him when he died. That must have been very difficult for you."

"Yes," Sarah said politely, desperately wishing that the woman would change the subject. "It's kind of you to ask, but . . ."

"I understand you were alone with him for a while before Eli Wulfe arrived at the mine shack. A father reuniting with his child should have quite a bit to say about some important things."

"Please," Sarah said. "I appreciate your interest, but I would rather not talk about my father's death."

"Yes, Sybil," Mrs. Caulfield began, but Mrs. Morton's eyebrows raised, wiggled a moment, then settled into place. She would not let Sarah be.

"I was told that you were able to wound the man who shot your father," she persisted.

Mrs. Caulfield gave a small, whispery gasp.

The Caulfields' room faded around Sarah, the heavy fur-

32

nishings, the expensive gewgaws disappearing until all she could see was her father in her arms . . . his face pale . . . his shirt stained with blood. Tears flooded her eyes.

Thin, cool fingers entwined themselves in hers, and Sarah heard Violet Caulfield say, "That's enough, Mrs. Morton. You have made Sarah cry." In an obvious attempt to change the subject, she said, "Mr. Caulfield and I came to this area as prospectors. Did you know that?"

Sarah shook her head, trying to compose herself. It was difficult to picture Mrs. Caulfield as a prospector's wife.

"We first lived in a mine shack on Pine Ridge, on the route to Weston Pass," Mrs. Caulfield said. "Mr. Caulfield named the mine *The Fidelity*, but it was a failure. We abandoned that venture and next tried our luck in Bartlett Gulch at *The Sweet Violet*." She blushed. "The name did not bring us the luck for which Mr. Caulfield had hoped. Needless to say, I was thankful when he made the decision to return to the newspaper business."

"Your husband had been a journalist before coming to Leadville?" Sarah asked politely.

"Ah, yes, in Chicago, then Denver, and even though there were already five other newspapers in Leadville, Mr. Caulfield judged that there was room for one more."

Susannah glanced around the ornate room and said, "It's obvious he has been very successful."

"Yes, yes," Mrs. Caulfield said. Now that she had achieved her purpose, the fingers withdrew, a wispy handkerchief was thrust into their place, and Mrs. Caulfield shrank back into her corner of the sofa. Mrs. Morton's glare, which pinned Mrs. Caulfield in place, was all that kept her from becoming invisible.

Mrs. Morton wasn't about to allow herself to be defeated.

She cleared her throat, carefully choosing her words as she said, "I am sometimes accused of speaking out too bluntly, but my questions to Sarah grew only out of my sympathy. It's a sad thing when two fine young women lose both parents within a short period of time." She glanced at both Susannah and Sarah and added, "This is a rough and difficult town, and it would not surprise me if you wanted to leave it and return to your home. If you should need financial help, well . . . please do remember Mr. Morton's banking facilities."

"Thank you, but I'm already making payments on a loan from your husband's bank," Sarah said. "He was kind enough to lend me the money to pay Susannah's travel expenses to Leadville."

Mrs. Morton leaned back in her chair, her diamonds reflecting the light from the lamps as they sparkled on her chest. "That is one thing I don't understand, Miss Lindley," she said. "After your father died, wouldn't it have been better for you to return to Chicago, instead of bringing your sister here?"

Susannah stiffened, staring at Sarah, who struggled for the right words to say. But suddenly Mrs. Caulfield sat upright, her fingers twisted together until the knuckles were bleached of color. "Mrs. Morton," Violet Caulfield said firmly, "I insist that we choose another topic of conversation. I, for one, would like to discuss . . . um . . . the Tabor Opera House, which should soon be celebrating opening night— on the twentieth of this month, I believe."

Susannah spoke up quickly. "I can tell you something about the opera house. One of Mrs. Hannigan's boarders, Mr. Vonachek, told us that the Tabor Opera House will be the first building in Leadville to be lit inside with gas jets, and it will be heated by a furnace!"

"Think of that!" Mrs. Caulfield said, her cheeks regaining their color as she concentrated on Susannah.

"And instead of wooden chairs or benches, there will be real theater seats, made of cast iron and scarlet plush—more than eight hundred of them."

As Mrs. Caulfield murmured appreciatively, Susannah became even more enthusiastic. "Even the aisles will be carpeted, and artists have been hired to paint the ceiling with cherubs and flowers and ribbons."

Mrs. Morton, unwilling to be outdone, interrupted. "You probably don't know that J. B. Lamphere, one of the most talented scenic artists in the country, has left New York and Philadelphia to come to Leadville to paint glorious mountain scenes on the drop curtain and stage backdrops."

"My, my," Mrs. Caulfield said.

Mrs. Morton began to talk about Horace Tabor and his great wealth, and how he was now diverting some of his money into politics, practically supporting the Republican party single-handedly. "But I have heard," she said, "that the man is neglecting his marriage. With all his mining interests and building projects and now his work as lieutenant governor, poor Augusta . . ."

Sarah stopped listening to the conversation. Mrs. Morton might consider herself well-meaning, but she was still a busybody. It was with a great sense of relief that Sarah heard the sliding doors to the dining room open and looked up to see Jeremy smiling at her.

Much later, after Sarah and Susannah had returned to the boardinghouse and were curled under the quilts, waiting for their body heat to create a pool of warmth in the bed, Sarah thought about Mrs. Morton's peculiarly persistent questions.

The woman was probably just as demanding in everything she did, and for a moment Sarah felt a pang of sympathy for her husband; but Mrs. Morton was soon out of mind as Sarah thought of Jeremy and his amusing tales, which had kept everyone laughing the rest of the evening. Life with Jeremy would never be dull.

Sarah giggled aloud, and Susannah mumbled groggily, "I like him, too, but we have to get up early. Go to sleep."

Susannah was right, Sarah thought, as her mind drifted from the charming young man she'd just left to the warm, rugged one who would arrive in only a few hours to take her riding with him.

Susannah shook Sarah awake while it was still dark. "Clint's downstairs eating breakfast," she said. "He asked me to tell you to get moving."

Sarah chuckled and said, "That sounds like something he'd tell his cattle." She hopped out of bed and reached for her warmest clothes, hurrying to wash up and dress as her teeth began to chatter in the cold air.

Susannah stopped, her hand on the doorknob, and turned to face Sarah. "What cattle?" she asked. "Clint drives a stage."

"He used to be a cowboy and work for a rancher," Sarah explained. "He's only working as a driver in order to raise enough money to buy his own ranch."

Susannah nodded. "Well, that's in his favor, although starting a ranch will mean a lot of hard work, unless he hires plenty of help."

Sarah finished buttoning the cuffs on her dress. "He won't be able to afford much help the first few years," she said.

"That means he'll work long hours, and if he marries, so will his wife. I don't count that to his credit."

Sarah took her sister by the shoulders. "What are you doing?"

"I just want to be sure . . . that is, in case . . ."

"If you're thinking that I may marry Jeremy or Clint, let me tell you this. Love doesn't add and subtract and come up with the highest points. Love comes from the heart."

"How do you know so much about love?"

Sarah felt herself blushing and turned away. "You're right. I don't."

Susannah put a hand on Sarah's arm. "When you fall in love, Sarah . . . when *I* do . . . I don't want what happened to Mother to happen to us. I don't want our husbands to run away and leave us."

Sarah gave her sister a reassuring hug. "Don't stay angry with Father. Just think about the love and the happy times he *did* give us."

"You were older. You remember them more than I do."

"In a few years, when the right man comes along for you—" Sarah began, but Susannah interrupted.

"Who says I have to wait a few years?" Susannah retorted and pulled away.

"Susannah!" Sarah gasped, but her sister had thrown open the door and was running down the stairs.

As Clint had promised, there was only a thin crust of snow in the meadow, and the moon, low in the sky, was still bright enough to highlight the landscape in soft silvers and blacks. The horses, setting each foot down deliberately, picked their way across the meadow, leaving a trail of shadowy imprints, and occasionally Sarah could see smaller, shallower tracks of forest animals that had scooted across the snow.

From the nearest cluster of trees, an owl hooted softly, and from a distance another owl answered.

"Oh, Clint, it's so beautiful!" Sarah whispered.

From a spruce close to her head came a skittering sound. A branch rustled, and a clump of snow slithered off, landing with a plop on Sarah's shoulder.

Clint laughed as she jumped in surprise, and she held a finger to her lips. "This place belongs to them—to the creatures who live here. We're intruders."

He reined in Samson and motioned to Sarah to pull Lady to a stop. "Look across the way, to the ridge opposite," he said quietly. "Two elk have come out of the woods."

"They're watching us," Sarah whispered. "Maybe they're wondering what kind of strange animals we are."

Clint shook his head. "They're wary. If they're wondering anything, it's whether or not they'll end up on someone's supper table."

"That's horrible!" Sarah said.

"That's the way of it," Clint told her. "I've seen plenty of families kept from starving to death because they had enough wild game to last them over the winter."

The bull elk suddenly lifted his head high, then turned and bounded back into the woods, his cow following close behind him. "Something spooked them," Clint said. He turned in the saddle and surveyed the ground they'd covered. "I don't think it was us."

Sarah and Clint began to walk their horses along the line

of the trees, and as the sky grew lighter, the animals within the forest awoke. A pine squirrel paused on a branch to scold them; and a red fox, stark against the snow, flashed across their line of vision, his gleaming fur tipped by the first rays of sunlight.

"Sarah," Clint said, "yesterday, when we talked about our dreams, and you didn't know what yours was yet . . . well, my dream is big enough for both of us. Matter of fact, you're a part of—"

The violent crack of a rifle shook the air. Sarah heard the whistle of the bullet, then the splat as it slammed into the trunk of a nearby pine. Snow showered around her. "Get down!" Clint yelled. "Get behind the trees!"

Sarah pulled her right leg free and jumped from the side-saddle, stumbling into the thick stand of trees. She turned to see Clint with the reins of both horses in his left hand, the rifle he'd pulled from its saddle holster in his right. He'd backed into the shelter of the trees, facing the direction from which the shot had come.

"There he is," he said.

A rider, far enough away to be only a black silhouette, rode at a canter away from them, heading toward Leadville. Sarah trembled. "Could that have been Eli Wulfe?"

Clint looped the reins to a low branch and examined the trunk of the tree. "Eli'd have no reason to come after us. To his way of thinking, he settled his score." He put his arms around Sarah, and she gratefully leaned against him. "Whoever took that shot wasn't trying to hit either of us. It was way too high."

"Then why shoot?"

Clint frowned as he thought. "Some dang fool careless with a rifle . . . or maybe after some squirrel meat for

39

supper . . . I don't know. All it did was scare the h— . . . was scare us."

"Maybe that's what he wanted," Sarah said, her thoughts churning. "To frighten me, or warn me."

"Why?"

Sarah stepped back so that she could look directly into Clint's eyes. "I think that a few minutes ago you were getting ready to ask me to marry you," she began. Clint tried to speak, but Sarah shook her head and went on. "You can't. Not yet. I'm not free to think of marriage."

"Sarah, listen to me," Clint interrupted.

"No!" Sarah said. "You listen to me. There's something I must tell you." While Clint held her gaze intently, his blue eyes darkening, Sarah told him the steps she had taken to find her father and repeated every word her father had said. "I promised Father that I'd clear his name, and since I know wrongdoing is going on, then I have a duty to find out what it is and reveal it. You understand, don't you?"

Clint nodded. "I understand. Keeping a promise is a matter of honor."

"Oh, Clint!" Sarah cried, with such a sense of relief that her knees wobbled.

He held her shoulders, steadying her. "I'll do what I can to help you find that proof," he said. "And I'll keep my peace about what I feel for you until you give me the word, and that's my promise."

Sarah longed to fling her arms about him, but Clint took her hand and led her to the horses. Sarah had set the rules, and Clint had accepted them. He helped her to mount Lady, then swung into his own saddle on Samson.

As they rode back to Leadville, Sarah was aware that Clint's rifle remained close at hand and he was alert to every

40

movement, every sound. She studied his profile, admiring his strength and quiet determination. *Do I love him?* she asked herself. *Enough to want to spend the rest of my life with him, to work beside him, to bear his children?*

She pushed the thought from her mind, refusing to answer.

Chapter 5

◆　◆　◆

The ride back was peaceful, and Sarah was finally able to convince herself that the shooter had been only a fool who didn't know how to handle a rifle. So far, she hadn't been bothered or threatened, perhaps because no one had known that Father had told her about the proof.

Someone knew now. Maybe she shouldn't have been so quick to divulge Father's secret to Clint. Sarah hoped she hadn't made a mistake.

When she returned to Mrs. Hannigan's, there was so much bustle going on in the kitchen, with preparations for the box supper, that Sarah couldn't help but join in the excitement.

"You have enough food for ten boxes," Sarah said with a laugh as she helped Mrs. Hannigan wrap large squares of gold cake in linen napkins.

Susannah came into the room trailing needle and thread, lengths of ribbons, and bits of lace. She held up a rose made out of pink paper. "You were right. I found all sorts of beautiful things in your scrap bag," she told Mrs. Hannigan.

"I save everything," Mrs. Hannigan said. "You never know when it might come in handy."

Sarah laughed as she reached for a familiar peacock blue ribbon. "You must have rescued this from the hat I wore from Chicago to Leadville."

"The hat was a disaster," Mrs. Hannigan said, "but all the ribbon needed was a bit of a washing and a warm iron."

Susannah laid the decorations on the table and took the blue ribbon from Sarah's hand. "Oh, please, Sarah, may I use your ribbon on my box? It's such a perfect color and exactly what I want! Please?"

Sarah shrugged. "If you want it, it's yours."

"The roses and lace would suit you," Susannah said, holding them up. "I know! Why don't you let me decorate your box for you? I'll make it very feminine and beautiful."

Mrs. Hannigan, her eyes twinkling, turned from the basin, where she was cutting thick slabs of cold, roasted brisket of beef. "There'll be at least two young men bidding for Sarah's box, no matter if it's wrapped in old newspaper."

Sarah's face grew warm, and she concentrated all her attention on making a sharp, square corner on the napkin she was folding, but Susannah didn't pick up on Mrs. Hannigan's teasing. She bent her head over the lace, pleating it into a rosette. "It's going to be elegant," she said.

"Save the purple velvet ribbon for me," Mrs. Hannigan told her. "I've used it before. There's a certain blacksmith who likes my cooking and watches for that ribbon. He's pleasant enough company for an evening."

Susannah raised her head. "I thought you warned us not to say a word about which box was ours."

"That's right, but I'll be letting the purple ribbon do my talking for me."

44

When the boxes were finally packed and their lids attached firmly with the ribbons, Mrs. Hannigan gave Sarah and Susannah small cards and envelopes. "Write your name on the card, seal it inside the envelope, and tuck it carefully under the ribbon at one end so that it won't come loose."

They did as she instructed, then stepped back to admire the boxes. The wide, bright, purple velvet ribbon on Mrs. Hannigan's box certainly would not be overlooked. Sarah's box stood out, too, with the frills of lace ruffles, pink ribbon, and the large pink rose. But Susannah's box was simple, with its peacock blue ribbon neatly tied in a bow.

"You've given all of the beautiful decorations to me," Sarah said. "Wouldn't you like some lace for your box?"

"Your box *is* beautiful, isn't it?" Susannah said. "But I'm tired of sewing." She scooped up the scraps on the table and said, "I'm going upstairs to get dressed."

"Wear something warm," Mrs. Hannigan said. "The hall's like the theaters—warmed only by body heat."

Susannah hesitated. "Only one of the dresses I brought with me is fine enough to wear to a party. It's Mother's black silk," Susannah said. "It's a good fit, and I only had to alter it just a little to make it more stylish."

Sarah was surprised. "Isn't black a little old and drab?" Mother's good black silk dress had only a high-necked dickey of creamy lace to relieve the black. It was decidedly a dress for a mature woman, not a vibrant young girl.

"The dress is not too drab," Susannah said. "You'll be surprised. It's really very attractive."

Mrs. Hannigan glanced at the clock on the shelf. "Best get ready," she said. "It won't be long before Mr. Caulfield arrives."

By the time Sarah entered their bedroom, Susannah was

45

already wearing the black silk, and over it, tied with a large bow, an elbow-length pleated cape. Sarah stopped short and stared at her sister, then lifted the photograph of their mother from the bedside table. "It's the dress Mother wore in the photograph, isn't it? Take off the cape and let me see."

"I've already gone to a great deal of trouble in tying a perfect bow and adjusting the pleats in this cape," Susannah said.

"You're the image of Mother," Sarah said softly, her eyes still on the picture.

Susannah leaned on Sarah's arm to peer around her at the photograph. "How old was Mother when this photograph was taken?" she asked.

"She must have been about twenty-six or twenty-seven," Sarah answered. "I remember when Father took us to a photographer's to have our portraits made. I was just six years old, and you were still three. We were dressed in new clothes and rabbit-fur muffs, and Father wanted a photograph of us, too, but first the photographer took Mother's picture. The bright flash of powder and the noise frightened us, and we both cried. 'We'll get the girls' photograph made next time,' Mother told him."

"But there wasn't a next time, was there?" Susannah asked. She reached out and took the picture from Sarah, placing it back on the table. "Let's not talk about Mother and Father now. Let's talk about the party. I've never been to a party like this one! Mrs. Hannigan taught me some steps. She says I learn quickly."

Sarah unbuttoned her shirtwaist and shrugged out of it, watching, amused, as Susannah leaned into the mirror and pinched her cheeks until they were rosy.

46

"I'll wait downstairs," Susannah said. "You'll have more room to dress." She pulled her heavy coat from the wardrobe and disappeared in a whirl of black silk.

By the time Sarah came downstairs, dressed in her blue wool with lace collar, Jeremy had arrived. As he was greeting Sarah, Mrs. Hannigan marched in, carrying the three decorated boxes, which immediately caught Jeremy's interest.

"Now, there's no telling secrets as to which box is which," Mrs. Hannigan admonished. As Susannah reached over to adjust the lacy frill around the pink rose on Sarah's box, smiling up at Jeremy, Mrs. Hannigan tapped her hand. "And there's no giving hints, either," she said.

Jeremy's eyes sparkled as he looked at the women's handiwork. "I remember that blue ribbon," he said to Sarah. "I'm surprised it survived. From the time we left Chicago, your poor hat had trouble staying on your head."

"Through no fault of my own," Sarah teased. She pulled on her new hat and gloves and scarf, as the others bundled up, and they hurried out to the carriage Jeremy had borrowed from his uncle Chester.

Sarah saw Clint the minute she entered the hall. He was waiting just inside the door, near a table where the men were checking their holsters and guns. He stepped forward as he spotted her. "I need to talk to you, Sarah," he said.

But Susannah called, "Clint, look at our boxes. Aren't they pretty?" She reached out to straighten one of the lace rosettes but Mrs. Hannigan snatched the boxes out of reach.

"Susannah! No giving away secrets!"

Susannah shrugged, her eyes wide and innocent. "I worked very hard on that box. I want it to look just so."

Mrs. Hannigan left them, carrying the boxes to be displayed on the long table of boards over sawhorses. Sarah

47

was less concerned with the boxes than she was with the challenging glare that passed between Clint and Jeremy. Jeremy helped Sarah and Susannah remove their coats, which he hung on the coat rack next to the door. Trying to distract him, she asked, "Jeremy, will you please take Susannah's cape, too?"

Susannah hugged the little cape closer and stepped out of Jeremy's reach. "No thank you. I'm going to leave it on for a while," she said. "It's chilly in here."

As other party guests hurried in the door, a woman with a red, white, and blue hostess badge pinned to her chest swept toward them, handing to each of the women small pencils, programmes for the evening's dances, and small dance cards attached to looped cords to hang around the wrist. Sarah, Susannah, Clint, and Jeremy walked together past the wooden chairs that lined the walls, pausing near the platform where the musicians were setting up their chairs and instruments. Desperately conscious of the mounting antagonism that passed between the two men, Sarah opened her programme. "Twenty-four dances!" she exclaimed. "Starting with a grand march!"

"By rights, your partner for the grand march should be your escort," Jeremy told her. "Miss Lindley, will you please pencil my name in your dance card?"

"You escorted three of us," Sarah teased. "How are you going to manage this?"

"I think Mrs. Hannigan's spoken for," Susannah said. "Look over there. A gray-haired gentleman with a thick gold watch chain has just offered her his arm."

Jeremy tucked Sarah's right hand firmly into the crook of his elbow. "I'm sure Clint will be glad to escort Susannah."

"What do you have to do in a grand march?" Clint asked, shifting from one foot to the other.

Jeremy grinned. "It's a march, that's all. All the partners just walk around the room until the music stops."

"I guess I can manage that," Clint said. He smiled at Susannah. "If you'll be my partner for that marching thing, I'll be honored."

Susannah beamed at Clint. Sarah offered him a warm smile of gratitude and relief.

As the musicians began to tune their instruments, three young men appeared at Sarah's side. "May I have a dance, ma'am?" "Will you pencil my name in your dance card?" "Are you free for the second?" they asked.

"The second has been given to Mr. Barnes," Sarah said, as she wrote in Clint's name, "but you may have the fourth, sir, and you the fifth . . ."

"Just a minute, Sarah. Don't leave me out," Jeremy interrupted as he leaned over her shoulder. He pointed. "Write me in here, here, and here."

"I'll remove this cape," Susannah said to no one in particular, "as soon as I take a quick look at the boxes."

As Susannah returned, Sarah noted the sudden silence in the group around her and raised her head, following their gaze toward her sister.

Susannah had altered Mother's dress, indeed. The entire lace dickey and collar had vanished, leaving a scooped neckline which, technically, did not break the laws of modesty, yet left no doubt that Susannah was amply filled out in the right places. Her waist had been cinched in so tightly that a large man might encircle it with his two hands, and the silk skirt swayed gracefully over her hips.

49

"Well!" Sarah said.

"Well, well," Jeremy murmured.

"Ma'am!" one of the men cried. He stumbled over his own feet, trying to elbow out the others who were heading for Susannah. "May I have the honor of a dance?"

As other men joined the group around the Lindley sisters, Clint squeezed in and said to Sarah, "When you get through writing down all those names, there's something I need to tell you."

"Tell me during the second dance. It's a quadrille," Sarah said.

"What's a quadrille?"

"I have no idea, so we can sit it out and talk." She grinned. "I put you down for the third dance, too. That's a waltz, and easy to learn. That one you *must* dance with me."

"Are you going to insist on it?"

"Yes."

"I don't think I'm cut out to be a dancer. I may tromp all over your feet."

"I don't mind."

He shrugged. "I'll do whatever will make you happy, Sarah."

She had no time to answer. The Master of the Dance stepped to the center of the platform and welcomed everyone to the party. He then announced that the auction for the box suppers would commence at the intermission, after the twelfth dance.

The band went into a lively grand march, and Sarah was swept onto the floor. As the party-goers paraded in a large circle, Jeremy leaned close and whispered to Sarah, "You're the most beautiful woman in the room."

Sarah *felt* beautiful. It was her first dance, her dance card was filled, and she was going to have a wonderful evening.

At the end of the march, a young man rushed up to claim Susannah, and Clint took Sarah's hand, leading her to a far corner of the room, where they sat on a pair of the wooden chairs. The music began, and Sarah watched Susannah, her cheeks pink with excitement, bow gracefully to her partner.

"Mrs. Hannigan must have been a good dance instructor, because Susannah's having a lovely time." Sarah smiled as she gave a mock sigh. "Not that I feel I could take responsibility for my younger sister's welfare, she seems not to need me at all, and if she did, I doubt she'd accept my help."

"Don't worry about it," Clint said. "I'd say that plenty of others around here will be glad to help you look after her." The expression on Clint's face grew more serious. "Sarah," he said, "I found out something today from the clerk at the rooming house where your father lived. Remember, you said he told you somebody came by and went through that box of things that belonged to your father?"

"Yes, but he couldn't remember who the man was. He didn't know his name."

"He does now. It came to him while we were talking about it."

"That's amazing!" Sarah said. "He wasn't the least bit cooperative while I was questioning him."

Clint cleared his throat and mumbled, "I might have questioned him a little differently than you did."

"Clint!" Sarah said. "You didn't . . . ?"

"I can say *please* and *thank you* as nice as anybody else," he answered, "but once in a while the time comes when that's not enough."

Sarah wanted to protest, but Clint had accomplished what she could not. "What did he tell you?"

"The man who looked through your father's things goes by the name of John Dunlap. I know him by sight. He works for Wilbur Owens, at Owens' Faro Club, watching the tables, sometimes tending bar, sometimes just being Owens's flunky."

"Why would he be concerned with Father's possessions?" Sarah thought about the rooming house where Father had lived—its small, dirty lobby and the rude, bored clerk who didn't want to answer her questions. "The clerk said after Dunlap had looked through the things in the box, he threw it down. Apparently he didn't take anything, and he seemed disappointed."

"Maybe he'd been looking for the same thing your father told you about. You see what that means, don't you?"

Sarah slowly nodded. "It probably means that no one has found Father's proof yet." Her hands were cold, and she grasped Clint's for support. "And they're wondering who has it."

Clint's fingers curled around hers, warming and strengthening them. "Just keep telling yourself, Sarah, we're the ones who are going to find it—not Owens and not anybody else."

We, Sarah thought, comforted by the knowledge that Clint was willing to help her.

The music stopped, and the Dance Master called for the third dance, a waltz. Sarah stood and pulled Clint to his feet.

"You're sure you want to go through with this?" he asked. "I don't own a pair of fancy dancing shoes, and my boots might be kind of heavy on your toes."

She smiled. "Put your right hand on my waist, and with your left hand hold my right hand out, like this." When they were in position, she said, "Now, when the music starts, keep counting to three. Take a long step and two small ones. One, two, three . . . one, two, three."

The waltz began, and as they stumbled around the sidelines, out of rhythm with the music, Sarah realized that Clint was right. He would never make a dancer. "You win," she said. "We'll sit this one out."

Before long it was time to dance with Jeremy again. He was by far the best partner Sarah had all evening. With Jeremy the dance steps came easily to her. He led her through the schottische and Virginia reel, and she laughed aloud with sheer joy as he twirled her around the room to the music of a Strauss waltz. Her time with Jeremy was up too quickly.

Sarah was preparing to meet her next partner when a tall black-bearded man stepped in front of her.

"I come to claim this dance," he said.

Sarah frowned. "I gave this dance to a Mr. Peavey. You aren't Mr. Peavey."

The man grinned. "Not by a damned sight. Mr. Peavey is sittin' this one out. He give me his place."

Sarah took a closer look. She had seen those eyes and heavy eyebrows before. Where? Suddenly she remembered. The last time she'd seen them, those eyes had peered at her over a dirty bandanna mask as this man robbed the Missouri Pacific train.

Chapter 6

•   •   •

Sarah was sure of it. Those eyes. And that voice. She'd never forget it, either. The robber had tossed a silver dollar to the conductor as he left and called, "Have a drink on Jesse James!"

"You're not Jesse James either," Sarah blurted.

"You remember?" He grinned. "I like to have my fun."

Sarah took a step backward. "Who are you? What are you doing here?"

The music began, and the man nodded in what could have passed for a bow. "My name's Harley Emmett, and I'm stayin' only long enough for one dance, no more, no less. It's worth a hundred dollars to me just to dance with the lady who took a shot at Eli Wulfe."

As Sarah hesitated, Emmett's heavy eyebrows drew down into a scowl, and he said, "I don't take kindly to bein' turned down."

The dancers had begun to whirl to the rhythm of John Philip Sousa's "Only a Dream," and a few people threw puzzled glances at Sarah and Emmett, who stood in the mid-

55

dle of the dance floor. Harley Emmett was a dangerous man, and Sarah quickly decided that it was safer to go along with his request.

"I'll dance with you," she said. As he raised his arms, she took her position, and soon they were gliding across the floor.

"Surprised? I'm a good dancer, ain't I?" he asked.

Sarah nodded. "Why are you here?"

"I told you—I just like my fun." He grinned. "The marshal's lookin' for me," he said, "and it makes me laugh that I'm right under his nose."

They whirled a few more turns in silence before he added, "I want to talk about your pa, too. We wasn't exactly friends, but he done me a couple of favors. Ben Lindley warn't on the wrong side of the law. He was a decent man."

Sarah cringed to think that her father had had dealings with people like Harley Emmett. "I know," she said, trying to keep her feelings from showing.

Emmett nodded, satisfied, then went on. "You know about Eli Wulfe? Them Wulfe brothers was bottom of the barrel. They never had no use for each other. Never had no use for nobody, for that matter. Somebody had to sweeten the pot for Eli to want to go gunnin' for your father."

"Somebody paid him?"

"I figure."

Father had told Sarah that Eli was merely an executioner. "Who?" she asked.

"Iffen I knew, I'd a done somethin' about it."

As they danced closer to the table where the gun belts had been checked, Emmett said, "I tried to find Eli Wulfe myself just to settle the score, but he's gone into hidin', and no one's tellin' where he is, iffen they know. I'm gettin' outta this high country, goin' up Nebraska way, so in case Eli's still holed up somewhere around these parts—and I suspect he is—you watch out, you hear?"

"I hear," Sarah said.

"Thankee, ma'am, for the dance," Emmett said, displaying a row of crooked and broken brown teeth as he grinned wickedly. "It was a real pleasure." Sarah fought off a shudder. He stopped, made a bow, and pulled a packet of greenbacks from his inside coat pocket. "One hundred dollars for the volunteer firemen," he said, and handed the money to the astonished hostess. In one quick movement Emmett grabbed his gun and holster from the table, belted them on, covered them with a long, filthy sheepskin coat, and dashed from the hall.

"Weren't that Harley Emmett?" Sarah heard a man ask. "What was he doin' here, dancin' with one of our ladies?"

"Naw. Couldn't be," another man said.

But loudly enough to be heard above the music, a woman whispered, "If that *was* Harley Emmett, it don't surprise me. Look at the *lady* he was dancin' with. Ben Lindley's daughter. You know who her father was—shot a man in cold blood, he did."

The hostess and the small group of people with her stared at Sarah with undisguised curiosity. Sarah quickly turned away, so they couldn't see the anger that stained her cheeks. "In cold blood." Was that what they believed? Well, Sarah knew the truth. And as soon as she could solve the riddle her father left behind when he died, all of Leadville would know the truth, too.

Sarah looked around, trying to judge whether the rumor about Harley Emmett's visit would spread through the hall. Apparently the dance was more interesting than gossip, and most people hadn't seemed to notice Emmett's presence or recognize him. Even Jeremy and Clint, who were keeping a close eye on all Sarah's other partners, hadn't seemed to recognize the bandit.

As the waltz ended, the Dance Master invited the women to take chairs at the right-hand side of the room and the men to move to the left-hand side. Still a little shaky, Sarah chose a nearby seat, and Susannah slipped in next to her during the bustle and chatter. Sarah longed to tell Susannah about Harley Emmett and what he had said about their father, but Susannah surely would disapprove of Sarah's public contact with an infamous bandit.

Instead Sarah asked, "Are you having fun?"

"It's wonderful!" Susannah gave Sarah a quick glance from the corner of her eye. "You don't care about what I did to change Mother's dress?"

"Tonight you can be the most popular belle in Leadville," Sarah told her. "Just remember that tomorrow you go back to being fifteen years old."

Susannah opened her mouth to retort but thought better of it. "Sarah, you just can't imagine how much I worried about this party," she said. "I was so afraid that no one would dance with me, and that no one would bid for my box."

The auctioneer held up a box draped in bright red ribbons, and Sarah said, "Shhh! They're going to begin."

The bidding, which was spirited over the boxes brought by the younger women who were yet unmarried, caused a great deal of laughter, shy giggles, and more than a few blushes. Husbands bid for the boxes brought by their wives, but they endured some good-natured price raising by the auctioneer.

Mrs. Hannigan let out a whoop when Leadville's black-smith bid ten dollars for her box. "Last year he bid only five," she said to Sarah and Susannah, "but this year I let it slip that I'd put in an extra slice of gold cake."

"Well, well, here's a box that somehow got hid underneath another one," the auctioneer said as he held up both Sarah's and Susannah's boxes. "All right. We'll take bids on this top box first—this box with the blue, blue ribbon." His voice went into a singsong chant. "Purty ribbon from a purty gal, and we all know that purty gals are all good cooks. So what do I hear? One dollar? Who'll start with one dollar? One dollar . . . one dollar . . ."

"Five dollars!" Jeremy called out.

"Six!" Clint yelled.

"Seven!"

"Ten!"

The blue ribbon! They both thought they were bidding on Sarah's box! Sarah leaned toward Susannah to tell her what was happening. But Susannah was smiling, and a flush of excitement washed over her face as she eagerly watched the proceedings.

"Susannah!" Sarah gasped. "You *wanted* them to think that was my box, didn't you?"

Susannah lifted her chin a little higher. "What if I did? You can't have both Jeremy and Clint. Why shouldn't I have one of them?"

It wasn't just Clint and Jeremy who bid. Other men in the crowd began to catch on that with Clint and Jeremy so intent to win, the box must belong to Sarah. The amount bid kept growing higher.

"Twenty-five dollars!" someone yelled.

Susannah moaned. "That was Mr. Peavey!"

Clint, with a scowl on his face, dropped out, leaning against the wall with his arms tightly folded across his chest. Sarah wanted to run to him and reassure him, and tell him that things were not what they seemed, but all she could do was sit quietly, a little embarrassed by all this mistaken attention, while the bidding went on.

"Forty dollars!" the auctioneer said. "Once . . . twice . . . sold to Mr. Jeremy Caulfield!"

Forty dollars! Sarah thought with amazement. Half her monthly salary!

"Thank goodness Mr. Peavey didn't win it!" Susannah whispered.

Jeremy made his way toward the table to collect the box he had won. His expression was so triumphant that Sarah found it hard not to laugh in spite of her discomfort.

As Susannah stared at Jeremy, she mumbled, "Oh, Sarah, what if he's angry? I think I made a dreadful mistake. What shall I do?"

Sarah immediately forgave her sister. "Enjoy the joke," she said as she patted Susannah's hand. "Jeremy will. You'll see."

"What about you? You don't really mind, do you?"

"Not this time," Sarah said. But she did mind . . . a little. "Just don't pull any more tricks like that again."

The auctioneer pulled the envelope from the box and said, "Let's take a look at this card and see who Mr. Caulfield's supper partner will be. Ah, ha! It's Miss Susannah Lindley. Congratulations, Miss Lindley. We never had nobody's box bring in this much. You set a record."

Sarah did laugh—she couldn't help it—at Jeremy's open-mouthed astonishment. But he quickly recovered, paid for the box, and carried it to Susannah. Offering his arm, he said, "I hope you don't have any more tricks up your sleeve, Susannah. There *is* food in this box, isn't there?"

"Mrs. Hannigan's finest," Susannah said.

As Susannah rose with a smile and took Jeremy's arm, Sarah was glad that it had been Jeremy who'd been taken in by Susannah's trick and not Clint. Jeremy had handled the situation with his usual charm, and Sarah had to admit to herself that Clint most likely would not have been quite as good-natured about it.

Clint was Clint, blunt and direct with little social polish; but he smiled across the room at Sarah, his good humor restored, and she gladly smiled back. She'd tell him about Harley Emmett—and she would tell Jeremy, too—but not tonight.

As the auctioneer chose his next box, Sarah's thoughts drifted from the front of the room, and Emmett's words came to her mind. If someone had paid Eli Wulfe to kill Father, it would have to have been a person who wouldn't handle a gun himself. He might be a man working in law enforcement who'd gone over to the other side. He could be someone prominent in Leadville, or a man too cowardly to come out of the shadows.

The auctioneer held up the box decorated in pink ribbon and lace. Sarah saw with a start that it was hers and began to pay attention. Bidding was active until Clint again ran out of money and good humor, and Mr. Peavey—more persistent than before—won the box with a bid of twenty-five dollars.

Sarah decided that she wasn't fond of box suppers. While she smiled and nodded and listened to Mr. Peavey's chatter, she kept an eye on Clint, wondering a little jealously who his supper partner would be. With great relief she saw him paired off with a woman at least twice his age, if not more; and she realized that she probably would have been somewhat jealous of Jeremy's partner, too, if he hadn't been safely matched with Susannah.

Gratefully Sarah saw the musicians return to their platform. She patted her lips with her napkin, gathered Mrs. Hannigan's other linens, and tucked them into the empty box. Politely she said, "Mr. Peavey, I have enjoyed your company, and your discourse on fur-farming experiments in Canada has been both instructive and fascinating. However, it's time for the dancing to begin, and I have promised the next dance to Mr. Caulfield."

"It has been a real pleasure," Mr. Peavey said. He stood and took Sarah's hand, helping her to her feet. "I would like to call on you, Miss Lindley. May I have your permission?"

Sarah saw Jeremy step up behind Mr. Peavey. He didn't say a word. He simply waited and listened for Sarah's answer, mischief lighting his eyes.

"You see, Mr. Peavey," Sarah began, not wanting to say anything that might encourage and then disappoint him, "I can't . . . that is, I would like to give permission, but . . . oh, dear, I . . . I'm sorry, but I'm not available."

"I see," Mr. Peavey answered stiffly. Sarah knew that her awkward rejection had wounded him, but she was still unused to all this attention from gentlemen, and she was entirely unpracticed at discouraging them. Jeremy stepped forward, holding out an arm for Sarah, and Mr. Peavey suddenly became aware of him. "I *see*," he said with greater emphasis, and—with a brief nod—scuttled away.

The Master of the Dance took his place again and called for the crowd to ready themselves for a Virginia reel. As

Sarah put her box back on the table, Jeremy followed her closely. He took her hands, swung her around, and searched her face. The mischief had left his eyes, and they were darkly serious as he asked, "Is there a reason why you're not available, Sarah?"

"I'm not available to Mr. Peavey," Sarah said, looking down to escape his meaningful gaze. "I know I lied, but I thought I could avoid hurting his feelings."

The members of the band began to tune their instruments, and Jeremy bent down to speak in Sarah's ear. "It doesn't have to be a lie," he said eagerly. "Come away with me, Sarah. I'll buy you a wedding ring finer than any you've ever seen. Think of all the worlds we can explore together! Wherever we go, I'll write my books and you'll write your poetry. . . . It may be in a grass hut on a sandy beach, or on the deck of a ship under sail, or perhaps on the back of an elephant!"

The spark in his eyes was contagious. Sarah felt her heartbeat quicken. At another time she might have been delighted by this extraordinary turn of events. For now, however, her promise to her father weighed so heavily on her that it was impossible even to consider what Jeremy asked of her. "Jeremy, I can't run away," she said softly.

"Why not?"

"Because I have responsibilities."

"We don't need responsibilities," Jeremy said. "We need each other. Think about it, Sarah. You and I . . ."

"No." Sarah held up her hand as he started to protest again. "My father was murdered because he had learned about some criminal activity taking place in Leadville. He told me he had proof, but he died before he could tell me where he'd hidden it." She took a deep breath. "Jeremy,

I promised Father I would find his proof and bring the criminals to justice. I promised Father I would clear his name."

"Oh, dear, little Sarah," Jeremy said, "there are more criminals in Leadville than anyone could count, and most of them will *never* be brought to justice. Don't try to live in the past. Think about today. Think about the future."

"But I promised Father," Sarah began.

Jeremy interrupted. "Your father loved you. He'd never hold you to a promise that would be impossible to keep."

"But I loved him, and . . ."

"He'd want you to be happy." Jeremy smiled and bent close. "I can make you happy, Sarah."

"Take your places, ladies and gents," the Master of the Dance called out.

"Please, Jeremy, do as I ask," Sarah pleaded. "You must not ask me to marry you."

Jeremy laughed. "I'll ask again and again. You can't discourage me, Sarah. I . . ." A blast of music from the band drowned out the rest of his words.

A woman leaned toward Sarah and shouted, "Hurry. Take your places. We're ready to begin." The Master of the Dance began to call out the steps of a reel, and the couples responded, Sarah stepping forward to bow to her partner. Her body carried easily by the rhythm of the dance, Sarah allowed her mind to wander to a daydream of a life with Jeremy. A life filled with laughter and adventure was certainly tempting—and a far cry from the life she had been living only a few months ago, scrubbing floors and being ordered around like a servant by Uncle Amos and Aunt Cora in her own home.

As Sarah had told Jeremy, she could not even begin to make such a decision until she had kept her promise to her father. But in the meantime there was no harm that she could see in a little dreaming.

Chapter 7

◆　◆　◆

A week after the volunteer firemen's fund-raiser, Jeremy invited both Sarah and Susannah to the November 20 grand opening night of the Tabor Opera House.

"Yes, yes, yes!" Susannah cried, clapping her hands. She gave one small jump, then remembered her claim to adulthood and tried to appear sedate.

Sarah was glad for the invitation. It would be a welcome distraction. Clint had taken a stageload of passengers down to Denver, and the weather had closed in behind him. Sarah had no idea when he'd return, and she found that she missed him. At least for a time she wouldn't have to worry about any antagonism between her two suitors.

"Don't do any investigating until I get back here," Clint had cautioned Sarah before he left. "It's too dangerous— especially if that skunk Harley Emmett was right and someone paid Wulfe to kill your father." For a moment Clint's face had darkened, and Sarah could see that he was still angry that the outlaw had dared to insist on a dance with Sarah. But there had been a second part to Clint's warning.

"The clerk at your father's rooming house must have talked about what he told me, because he's gone, and John Dunlap's nowhere to be found. Nobody's seen a one of 'em. They either left Leadville or . . ."

Clint didn't need to finish the sentence. Sarah knew what he meant, and she was well aware that by confiding in Clint she'd put him in danger, too. It was probably just as well that she had not related the entire story to Jeremy.

"Sarah!" The impatience in Susannah's voice shook Sarah back to the present. "Stop daydreaming and listen to what Jeremy's telling us."

Jeremy's smile was indulgent. "Sarah's probably picturing the interior of the opera house and wondering if our seats will be in the back row or behind a pillar."

"Oh, no! I wasn't," Sarah began, then realized Jeremy had been teasing.

"Tabor brags that there are no bad seats in the house," Jeremy said. "Ours are right down front, because I'll be writing a report on the performance for *The Leadville Daily Star*."

"Then you're a celebrity, too," Susannah said.

Jeremy had the good grace to preen only a little. "It's going to be a special program," he told them, "with two plays. One's a short comedy, called *Who's Who?* but the other's the three-act *A Serious Family*, which was first performed in London. And J. S. Langrishe, who I'm told is a favorite Colorado comedian, will be the opening act."

"You have a fascinating job," Sarah remarked. "Every day it's something new."

Jeremy grinned. "Yes, it is. I've even learned to set type on a Washington handpress. It's interesting, and so is the interviewing, but the writing is what I like best." He quickly amended what he said. "That is, *some* of the writing. Believe

68

ordered around like a servant by Uncle Amos and Aunt Cora in her own home.

As Sarah had told Jeremy, she could not even begin to make such a decision until she had kept her promise to her father. But in the meantime there was no harm that she could see in a little dreaming.

Chapter 7

◆　　◆　　◆

A week after the volunteer firemen's fund-raiser, Jeremy invited both Sarah and Susannah to the November 20 grand opening night of the Tabor Opera House.

"Yes, yes, yes!" Susannah cried, clapping her hands. She gave one small jump, then remembered her claim to adulthood and tried to appear sedate.

Sarah was glad for the invitation. It would be a welcome distraction. Clint had taken a stageload of passengers down to Denver, and the weather had closed in behind him. Sarah had no idea when he'd return, and she found that she missed him. At least for a time she wouldn't have to worry about any antagonism between her two suitors.

"Don't do any investigating until I get back here," Clint had cautioned Sarah before he left. "It's too dangerous—especially if that skunk Harley Emmett was right and someone paid Wulfe to kill your father." For a moment Clint's face had darkened, and Sarah could see that he was still angry that the outlaw had dared to insist on a dance with Sarah. But there had been a second part to Clint's warning.

"The clerk at your father's rooming house must have talked about what he told me, because he's gone, and John Dunlap's nowhere to be found. Nobody's seen a one of 'em. They either left Leadville or . . ."

Clint didn't need to finish the sentence. Sarah knew what he meant, and she was well aware that by confiding in Clint she'd put him in danger, too. It was probably just as well that she had not related the entire story to Jeremy.

"Sarah!" The impatience in Susannah's voice shook Sarah back to the present. "Stop daydreaming and listen to what Jeremy's telling us."

Jeremy's smile was indulgent. "Sarah's probably picturing the interior of the opera house and wondering if our seats will be in the back row or behind a pillar."

"Oh, no! I wasn't," Sarah began, then realized Jeremy had been teasing.

"Tabor brags that there are no bad seats in the house," Jeremy said. "Ours are right down front, because I'll be writing a report on the performance for *The Leadville Daily Star*."

"Then you're a celebrity, too," Susannah said.

Jeremy had the good grace to preen only a little. "It's going to be a special program," he told them, "with two plays. One's a short comedy, called *Who's Who?* but the other's the three-act *A Serious Family*, which was first performed in London. And J. S. Langrishe, who I'm told is a favorite Colorado comedian, will be the opening act."

"You have a fascinating job," Sarah remarked. "Every day it's something new."

Jeremy grinned. "Yes, it is. I've even learned to set type on a Washington handpress. It's interesting, and so is the interviewing, but the writing is what I like best." He quickly amended what he said. "That is, *some* of the writing. Believe

68

me, writing about the opening of the Tabor Opera House is greatly preferable to writing about the criminal element in Leadville."

Sarah shuddered. "If they wrote about every crime that took place in this town, it would fill all six newspapers."

"You wrote the story about that barber who got robbed on State Street, didn't you?" Susannah asked.

"Yes," Jeremy answered. "Carl Bockhaus. He was taking home a great deal of money—the day's receipts—when two men tried to hold him up. Mr. Bockhaus defended himself and shot and killed one of them—a man who was wanted for robbery in Texas. The other one—a Mr. Patrick Stewart—is now in jail."

"Mr. Vonachek told us that a mob formed outside the jail," Susannah said. "They talked about pulling Mr. Stewart out of jail and lynching him, and Edward Frodsham, too. He got arrested yesterday, and Mr. Vonachek said that Mr. Frodsham's the worst of all the lot jumpers."

Sarah remembered the brutality of the lot jumpers she had seen. Had one of them been Edward Frodsham? She gripped Susannah's hand, not so much to reassure her sister as to bolster her own courage. "Don't worry. The good people of Leadville won't lynch anyone. Lynching is murder."

"But not when they're lynching a criminal. Mr. Vonachek told us that Mr. Frodsham went to prison for murder in Wyoming, but somehow he got a pardon and soon afterward killed a man in Laramie. Mr. Frodsham claimed it was self-defense, and he got off and came to Leadville."

"Listen to me, Susannah. It doesn't matter what the crime was. Everyone deserves a fair trial."

"The criminals aren't being fair to the citizens."

"Nevertheless, there won't be any lynchings in Leadville,"

Sarah insisted, but she looked to Jeremy to add his support. "Will there, Jeremy?"

For a change Jeremy's expression was solemn. "I don't know," he said. "Like you, Sarah, I can only hope not."

Susannah arose earlier than usual on Thursday morning, the twentieth of November. As she dressed, her movements awoke Sarah.

"I can't help it," Susannah explained. "I've waited for this day for a long time. I'm so excited. Everyone is talking about the Tabor Opera House. It's supposed to be more grand than anything in Denver—in all of the West." She thought a moment. "Maybe even Chicago."

Susannah rattled on while Sarah dressed. Mr. Vonachek had told her this or that about the opera house and the actors who had arrived on the stage. She repeated every scrap of information, but Sarah paid her little attention.

Weston Pass was open again, and Sarah hoped that Clint would soon drive his stagecoach back to Leadville. The night before, she had finally talked to Susannah about what Harley Emmett had said and about Clint's information concerning John Dunlap's disappearance. Unfortunately Susannah had merely pointed out another dead end in the search. "Harley Emmett was only guessing, and the clerk and Mr. Dunlap have probably left Leadville and won't be of any help to you. Sarah, why can't you forget your promise to Father? You'll never be able to carry it out, or you'll be old before you do—too old to marry anyone. And you know it's only right and proper for an older sister to marry before a younger sister."

Sarah had hoped her initial astonishment didn't show. Since the dance a number of young men had called to see

70

Susannah, but their visits hadn't lasted long, and Susannah had discouraged them from coming back. She'd offered a series of complaints—one was too young, one too old, one too boring, and so on. She'd refused to receive Mr. Peavey at all. Sarah was grateful to see that Susannah was so choosy. She was much too young to even begin thinking about marriage.

But now it occurred to Sarah that perhaps she hadn't paid close enough attention. Maybe there was another reason Susannah had rejected all those callers. Maybe there was someone of whom Susannah approved. Sarah had asked, "Just who is it you're thinking of in terms of marriage?"

Susannah had looked away and shrugged, but Sarah had persisted, although she was a little afraid of hearing the answer. "Has anyone asked?"

"Not yet, but he will."

"Who is he, Susannah?"

"Never you mind," Susannah had said, her lower lip curling into a stubborn pout. "Just give some thought to what I told you."

Trying to ease the situation, Sarah had teased, "I know! It must be Mr. Peavey! It has to be!"

"Sarah!" Susannah's sharp voice brought Sarah back to the current conversation. "You're daydreaming again. I don't think you heard a word I said."

"Of course I did," Sarah told her. "I'll go downstairs with you and lend you a hand." She walked behind Susannah, who carried the oil lamp, lighting wall sconces on the stairs and in the parlor on her way.

The wood fire in the kitchen stove had been started, and water set to boiling, before Mrs. Hannigan bustled into the room, nervously clenching and unclenching her hands. "I

71

tapped on Mr. Vonachek's door to awaken him—as I do every morning, rain or shine—and when he didn't answer, I peeked through the door to make sure he was all right. He wasn't there. His bed hasn't been slept in."

"He was with us here last evening," Sarah said.

"I know he was. So what could have happened to him?"

Suddenly there was a scuffling noise at the back door. Mrs. Hannigan hurried to open it, and Mr. Vonachek stumbled in. He wore no hat, his scarf was awry, and his hands shook as he fumbled with the buttons on his coat, trying to unfasten them.

Mrs. Hannigan's eyes were wide. "Where have you been?" she asked.

"I went for a walk," he mumbled.

"In the dark? In this cold? Here . . ." She pulled at his arm. "Come over by the stove. It's the warmest place in the house."

"I'll help you with your coat," Sarah said. She unfastened the last two buttons and tugged it from his shoulders. Mr. Vonachek was shaking, and his arms were stiff, but Sarah managed to remove the coat.

The pointed toe of her right shoe caught on something, and she glanced down to see a small wad of black cloth. While Mrs. Hannigan and Susannah huddled over Mr. Vonachek, trying to care for him, Sarah picked up the cloth and shook it out. It was a hood—a black hood. Silently, not daring to wonder what the evil-looking hood was doing in Mr. Vonachek's possession, Sarah tucked it down deep inside one of his coat pockets.

She walked around Susannah and Mrs. Hannigan to stand in front of Mr. Vonachek. "Something has upset you terribly. Do you want to tell us about it?" she asked.

72

He stared at Sarah for only a few seconds before his resolve seemed to crumble. "Vigilantes dragged two men from the jail and hanged them," he answered.

Susannah gasped, and Mrs. Hannigan stepped back with a cry.

Mr. Vonachek's face was as white as the snow piled outside on the window sill, and the hollows around his eyes were so dark that Sarah felt nothing would ever erase them. "Undersheriff Watson . . . he was taken by a group of vigilantes who wore hoods over their faces and heads." Mr. Vonachek's throat muscles worked with difficulty, and his voice rasped like fingernails on slate. "They led Watson to the jail, which was locked on the inside, and told him to call out so those inside would open the doors. Once the doors were open, the vigilantes rushed in and overpowered the jailers and pulled those two men—Stewart and Frodsham—out of their cells. Edward Frodsham put up a terrible fight." Mr. Vonachek shuddered and swayed on his chair, closing his eyes.

"Would you like a glass of water, Mr. Vonachek?" Sarah asked.

His eyes snapped open, and he went on as though he hadn't heard her question. "The vigilantes carried them off to a building under construction on Harrison Avenue, and that's where they hanged them," he whispered. "Right over the rafters. Their bodies are swinging there now."

Susannah cried out, but Mrs. Hannigan said, "We should have expected it. Someone had to do something. Leadville couldn't keep going on the way it was headed."

Mr. Vonachek struggled to his feet. "I—I'm going upstairs to lie down," he said, and turned toward the back stairway.

They waited until he had stumbled out of earshot. "He

73

must have been one of them," Mrs. Hannigan whispered, "with all that talk of his about the Merchants Protective Patrol. And he was out all night."

"What will happen to the vigilantes?" Susannah asked.

"If their identities are made known, they'll be arrested for murder," Sarah answered.

"That's not fair!"

"Neither is murder."

"Never mind." Mrs. Hannigan patted Susannah's shoulder. "Under the circumstances those who have any information will keep it to themselves. No harm will come to Mr. Vonachek. Isn't that right, Sarah?"

Sarah thought about that black hood. It was not proof that Mr. Vonachek had actually taken part in the hanging. She thought about the crimes she had seen, the footpads who had assaulted her, and the gun she had to carry for protection.

"We can only believe what Mr. Vonachek told us," she said. "He described what he *saw*. He didn't say he took part in it."

Mrs. Hannigan nodded with satisfaction. "He also said that the bodies were still hanging." She looked toward the door, then back to Susannah. "You can handle the breakfast alone, can't you?" she asked. "People will be talking about this for months—maybe years, and I must go and see it for myself. Or would either of you girls like to go, too?"

"No!" Sarah said firmly, not even willing to give her sister the choice. "Susannah and I will make the breakfast."

After Mrs. Hannigan had left the room, Susannah threw Sarah a resentful glance. "I didn't want to go. I would have told her so," she said.

"Of course you would have," Sarah said.

74

"I mean you didn't have to speak for me. You're not my mother."

Sarah gave her sister a quick, reassuring smile and said, "We'd better hurry. The other boarders will soon be down for breakfast."

As Sarah left the schoolhouse that afternoon, Jeremy was there to meet her, excitement glowing in his face. "I was there, Sarah! I wrote a good part of the story! Uncle assigned two of us to work on it."

"Were you with the vigilantes, Jeremy?" Sarah asked.

Jeremy didn't notice her tension as he went on. "Someone came pounding on Uncle's door, and I dressed and raced to the scene. There were no pedestrians in sight, and my eyes were drawn to the two bodies twisting slowly in the cold night breeze. It was a grotesque scene: the bodies, a slew of black hoods scattered on the ground, and the gas lamps, flickering, flickering . . ." He stopped. "That's right from the story, just the way I wrote it. You'll read it soon. We got an extra edition of the newspaper out early. I even helped set type."

Sarah took his arm as they headed toward the edge of the street where the scraps of blackened snow had been hard-packed by wagon wheels. There wasn't as much traffic as usual, and Sarah commented on it.

"Many people are afraid to come out," Jeremy told her. "They're afraid there might be an outbreak of violence on one side or the other, and they're nervous about the detachment of militia stationed at the Clarendon Hotel. You did know the militia had been sent for, didn't you?"

"No, I didn't." Sarah was surprised, but not at the news of the militia. "What are you telling me, Jeremy? Do they

75

think there'll be more action from the vigilantes? Or are you saying that the criminal element might strike back?"

"It could be both," he said. "The note that was found pinned to Frodsham's back, after his body had been cut down, was a direct challenge."

"What note?"

Jeremy shoved a hand inside his heavy overcoat and fished into his jacket pocket. He pulled out some scraps of paper, looked through them, and read:

Notice to all lot thieves, bunko steerers, footpads, thieves, and chronic bondsmen for the same, and sympathizers for the above class of criminals: This shall be your fates. We mean business, and let this be your last warning . . . and a great many others known to this organization. Vigilantes' Committee. We are 700 strong.

"The message was followed by a list of undesirables who were encouraged to leave town," Jeremy told her. "Many of those individuals apparently decided that a quick departure was a good idea and must have left in a hurry, because there's been no sign of them." He paused, and Sarah could hear the satisfaction in his voice as he said, "I put that piece of news into my story, too."

Sarah carefully stepped over a slick patch of ice as she asked, "What is going to come of all this?"

"A better-controlled town, they hope. The city council has already wired Martin Duggan and asked him to return to Leadville and take over his old job of marshal."

"And in the meantime?"

"In the meantime life will go on as usual." They had reached the walk in front of Mrs. Hannigan's home, and

76

Jeremy paused. "The curtain will rise at eight-thirty, so I'll pick you and Susannah up at seven forty-five."

"Jeremy! After what's happened, surely the opera house will delay its grand opening!"

Jeremy shook his head. "The performers have been hired and have to keep to their schedule. Horace Tabor insists that the show must go on, so the grand opening will be held as planned."

"But the hanging took place just across the street from the Tabor Opera House. Doesn't that bother anyone but me?"

"It will probably upset a number of people. I doubt if the grand opening will be quite as grand as originally planned." He took her hands, and she could see the pleading in his eyes. "I've been assigned to cover the event, so I'll have to go, but you don't have to come with me if you don't want to."

"Of course I'll go with you," Sarah said. But in her mind she could picture the scene of the hanging—the framework of the unfinished building they would have to pass. The ropes that had been knotted around the necks of Patrick Stewart and Edward Frodsham still dangled across its rafters.

Sarah couldn't help but think of Father. If she did uncover his hidden proof of criminal activity and make it public, in such a lawless place as Leadville would anyone even notice or care?

Chapter 8

♦   ♦   ♦

As Sarah and Susannah prepared to leave with Jeremy for the grand opening festivities, Mrs. Hannigan put a protective arm around Susannah's shoulders. "Are you sure it's wise to go out on Harrison Avenue tonight, Mr. Caulfield?" she asked. "I've heard that most of the good folks in Leadville are staying indoors, where they feel at least a mite safer."

"There's nothing to worry about. There's a detachment of militia stationed right next to the opera house at the Clarendon Hotel and another on Chestnut Street," Jeremy said. "The local lawmen are on the alert, and the Merchants Protective Patrol will be on hand. I'll take good care of Sarah and Susannah." Mrs. Hannigan continued to look worried, so he assured her, "I'll be right at their side to protect them and see that they come to no harm."

Sarah tied the ribbons of her hat into a bow and pulled on her gloves. Even with Jeremy willing to take on any of the wrong-sided elements of society, the weight of the Colt derringer in her purse was reassuring. The opening of the opera house might be a special social occasion, but under the circumstances she wished that Jeremy had worn a gun.

"Then go and have a good time." Mrs. Hannigan sighed and said, "I guess I have no right to interfere, but these girls are like my daughters."

Jeremy did his best to distract Sarah and Susannah as they rode up Harrison Avenue toward the Tabor Opera House. There was much less traffic on the street than usual, and as they passed the building where the hanging had taken place, Sarah's glance turned toward it in spite of her resolution not to look in that direction.

In the yellowed light from the nearest gas lamp, the rafters were stark and bare, but Sarah could imagine the ropes and the two bodies that swung there. Almost directly across the street was the Clarendon Hotel. In front of the hotel a group of men in military uniform guarded a pile of weapons and ammunition. Whatever festive feeling Sarah may have had immediately vanished.

Susannah, however, calmly continued her conversation with Jeremy. "The hanging is over and done with," Susannah had told Sarah, "and whether it was right or wrong, there's no point in drooping around with sorrowful faces. Mr. Tabor wants to hold his grand opening, and it would be folly not to attend." She'd given Sarah a sideways glance and added, "I'm sorry that Mr. and Mrs. Caulfield won't be there. They're always so glad to see you, Sarah. You know, don't you, that they approve of you."

"Approve of me?" Sarah had laughed. "You mean as a bride for their nephew?"

Susannah had turned away so that Sarah couldn't see her face. "There's no need to laugh at what I said. The Caulfields are well respected in Leadville, and Jeremy will undoubtedly rise to a top position on *The Leadville Daily Star.* Think about it, Sarah. You'd never have to worry about making ends meet. It would be a good match."

Sarah hadn't answered, but Susannah's words had made Sarah think about Jeremy and her feelings for him. He was a friend . . . a very good friend . . . well, maybe more than a friend. Jeremy or Clint. Clint or Jeremy. This was a choice she wasn't ready to make.

As Jeremy held out a hand to help Sarah alight from the carriage, his glance met hers with so much warmth and affection that she melted. Susannah had been right about one thing. There should be no long faces at a festive celebration, and everything about the Tabor Opera House was festive.

The building was lit, both outdoors and in, with gas lamps. The deep red of the carpets and upholstered theater seats gave the room a rich glow, which rose from its brilliantly painted walls to its frescoed ceiling decorated with flowers and cherubs. On either side of the stage were two large proscenium boxes, carpeted and mirrored, with lace curtains offering privacy to the occupants.

"Oh, my!" Susannah cried. "I've never seen anything so beautiful!"

As soon as their coats and hats had been given to the attendant at the cloakroom, Jeremy proudly produced three tickets from his waistcoat pocket and presented them to an usher, who led them to seats in the third row, center, and handed them programmes.

Some other theatergoers had already arrived, and guests continued to trickle in, but as it grew closer to the time for the curtain to rise, Sarah noticed many vacant seats. The vigilante action had a chilling effect on Leadville as the inhabitants of the city waited and wondered what would happen next.

"Look, Sarah!" Susannah, who sat on Sarah's right, tugged at her arm. "Some people were just seated in the box on our right. Who are they?"

Jeremy leaned across Sarah to whisper, "Horace and Augusta Tabor, and some of their friends. I recognize a state senator, but I don't know the others."

"We're in important company!" Susannah exclaimed, her eyes shining.

This was a glorious, fantasy-filled evening, and Jeremy seemed very much a part of it. Sarah couldn't help compare Jeremy to Clint—dear, blunt, wonderful Clint—who would be so ill at ease in these surroundings.

The members of a fifteen-piece orchestra, each dressed in red-and-gold band uniforms, marched into a circular box below the stage and seated themselves. Susannah wiggled with anticipation. "It's going to begin . . . any minute!"

Even though they were not playing to a filled house, at exactly eight-thirty the conductor raised his baton, and the music began. Ushers extinguished all the lights in the theater, with the exception of the footlights that ringed the front of the stage. A boy scurried to the stage and dimmed the gas jet in each footlight, but twice his fingers were too quick, and he accidentally snuffed out the gas. He had to run back with a long sulphur match and relight those lamps, turning them down with greater care.

The band played on until the boy had finished his chore, then to fanfare and enthusiastic applause, the comedian J. S. Langrishe strode onto the stage.

Under cover of the theater's darkness, Jeremy reached for

Sarah's hand and held it snugly and warmly; and even though Sarah was caught up in the laughter and the drama onstage, she was very much aware of Jeremy's presence beside her.

It was later than usual when Sarah left the schoolhouse the next afternoon. The thin rays of the sun had disappeared over the mountain peaks, and the sky was a smear of gray. She was eager to reach the warmth and comfort of Mrs. Hannigan's, but she stopped abruptly as she saw the shadows shift between two buildings she would have to pass. As her eyes became adjusted to the darkness, she could make out the shape of a man. He was standing quietly, facing her. Was he watching? Waiting for her to come nearer?

Against the snow she was more visible to him than he was to her. She'd learned to use that visibility to help herself. Deliberately, so that the man could see, Sarah removed the derringer from her purse, cocked it, and slowly brought it up, aiming in his direction.

Immediately the shadows closed in, and Sarah could hear footsteps thudding between the houses, as the man ran away.

Footpads! Apparently Thursday morning's hanging hadn't discouraged all of the criminal element in Leadville. Sarah held the gun tightly, unwilling to replace it in her purse, as it occurred to her that this might have been someone with more sinister intent than a footpad—someone who had been waiting just for her.

Sarah took a long breath to steady herself, kept her gun at her side, her finger on the trigger, and walked even more quickly toward home.

Her heart gave a jump as she saw Samson tied at the post in front of the house. Clint! His stage had returned to

Leadville! Sarah slipped her gun back into her purse and ran up the steps and into the house, nearly colliding with Clint just inside the door.

He needed a shave, his pants and boots were mud-stained, and his sheepskin coat smelled of sweat and horses, but Sarah didn't mind. "Sarah!" he shouted with relief, and grabbed her by the shoulders with so much energy that she stumbled and nearly lost her balance. "I was just going after you. I came here and not to the schoolhouse, because I thought you'd be home by now."

"It's my fault," Susannah said. She stepped from behind Clint, her expression contrite. "I didn't think to tell Clint that you hadn't come home yet, Sarah. There was so much he didn't know about what had happened while he was gone—the vigilantes, and the opening of the opera house, and . . ."

"Word about the hangings reached us on the trail," Clint interrupted, his eyes never leaving Sarah's face. "We met a few people who were clearing out of Leadville in a hurry, and they had a lot to say about what took place. The general opinion was that there'd be more violence—on both sides." He took a long, slow breath and said, "I was worried about you, Sarah."

"I'm all right," she said.

Susannah put a hand on Clint's arm. "Supper's almost ready," she told him. "We're having stewed chicken and dumplings, which I made myself. Why don't you take off your coat and come back to the kitchen and find out what a good cook I am?"

Clint smiled and rubbed his fingertips across his stubbled chin. "Not like this," he said. "I'm not fit company. I came directly here because I needed to make sure that Sarah . . . that both of you were all right."

Sarah saw her sister's disappointment and hurried to say, "Susannah *is* a good cook, Clint. She'll keep a generous portion warm for you if you want to come back."

"Will *you* be here? Or have you got other plans?"

"I'll be here."

Clint took a step closer, but Susannah laughed and said, "Better hurry up, Clint. I won't be able to keep the chicken and dumplings warm forever."

Sarah and Susannah stood at the front windows, the lace curtains pulled aside, watching Clint ride away.

"He's very handsome." Susannah gave a little start, as though she hadn't meant to speak her thoughts aloud, then added, "But, of course, he'll never be more than just a cowboy."

Sarah looked at her sister. "Clint will soon be a rancher. He'll have his own land and his own cattle."

Susannah shrugged. "All that means is that he'll just have to work harder. You can call it rancher, cowboy, or cowhand. It's still the same dirty, smelly, exhausting job."

"How do you know so much about it?"

"I asked Clint."

"When was that?"

"Oh, I don't know." Susannah looked away. "Maybe at the dance."

Sarah tried to push away the prickles of irritation. "You're not very subtle, Susannah, and I'd appreciate it if you'd stop trying to discourage any interest I have in Clint. What I decide to do is up to me alone, and no concern of yours."

Susannah's eyes widened. "All I did was ask him about

his plans to buy land for a ranch. After what you'd told me, I was simply curious, and it had nothing to do with you."

"Then I'm sorry that I spoke too quickly," Sarah apologized, although she was still dubious. "I must work out my own solutions to my problems and arrange my own life without interference."

"That's very interesting," Susannah answered, "especially since you have a great deal to say about what *I* do with *my* life!"

"That's different," Sarah told her. "You're my little sister. You're in my care."

"I have a job of my own and can take care of myself," Susannah snapped. "I'm not in your care."

"I *am* your older sister," Sarah said, "and even though you dress like a woman, you're only fifteen and still a child. I had no right these past months to expect you to take the responsibility for all practical matters. And I know now that I'm perfectly capable of doing so myself." Sarah tried to put an arm around her sister's shoulders, but Susannah pulled away and marched toward the kitchen.

She's used to having me follow her lead, Sarah admitted to herself. *And once I was perfectly willing to do so. But it's different now.*

She took a few steps after Susannah, getting as far as the dining room, before Mrs. Hannigan burst through the door to the kitchen, her arms filled with small covered baskets of warm bread. Sarah took some of the baskets from her, placing them around the table.

She turned toward the kitchen again, but Mrs. Hannigan stopped her by saying, "I take it, by the expressions on your faces, that you and Susannah exchanged a few cross words?"

"A few," Sarah said, "although I didn't mean them to

86

be." She sighed. "It's hard taking care of a fifteen-year-old girl who thinks she's grown to womanhood. I honestly don't know what she has in mind or what it is she wants."

"You've noticed it, too?" Mrs. Hannigan said.

"Noticed what?"

"That Susannah's got her mind set on something." She smiled. "Your sister's a dear girl, but I can see that when she goes after something she wants, there's no getting in her way."

Sarah nodded. "She's always been like that. Father laughed at Susannah's stubbornness, but Mother said a better word would be determination."

They both smiled, and Mrs. Hannigan put a hand on Sarah's shoulder. "Don't go to her now," she said. "Give her a chance to collect herself so there'll be no more angry words."

Sarah went upstairs to change and wash before supper. As an extra touch, maybe as an offer of peace, she pinned the little garnet-and-silver pin that Susannah had given her to the bodice of her dress.

As she returned to the parlor, a voice from the stairs called out, "Miss Lindley! Will you wait, please?" Mr. Vonachek hurried down the stairs and stood before her. He seemed very much his old self, and Sarah was thankful.

"Thank you for caring for me yesterday morning," he said. "It was kind of you and your sister to help me. I was terribly upset by what I had . . . seen."

Sarah remembered the hood that had fallen from his pocket and shuddered. "Yes. It must have been horrible," she answered. "The best thing you can do is try to forget it."

"I don't know how I can," he said, a stricken look coming

87

back to his eyes. "Do you know that there have been sight-seers? All day yesterday they were there, even though there was nothing to see; and this morning, when I went to my job at the courthouse, I saw them—people who had come just to gawk and talk about what had happened."

"Oh, Mr. Vonachek," Sarah pleaded, "I hope and pray there won't be any more action from the vigilantes. Murder is still murder, no matter who commits it."

"Yes," he said, and looked away. "I have come to agree with you."

Sarah sat at the end of one of the sofas, and Mr. Vonachek perched at the other. "Miss Lindley," Mr. Vonachek said, "your sister has told me about the temporary loss of your property in Chicago."

"I'm afraid it's not temporary," Sarah told him. "Our uncle and aunt simply moved in and took over."

"Ah, but they can be made to move out by legal means under certain conditions." Mr. Vonachek sat up a little straighter, his shoulders broadening with self-confidence. "With my background in accounting—specializing in property claims, disposition, and disputes—I consider myself quite knowledgeable about matters such as yours, and I shall be glad to make an appointment with you to discuss the proper steps that can be taken."

"Why, Mr. Vonachek," Sarah said, "that's exceedingly kind of you."

"It would mean your return to Chicago, of course," he said. "I'm sure that a return to that city would please you very much. I, myself, have been considering returning to a civilized society."

Sarah thought about Chicago. Her life there seemed to have taken place so long ago. Her happy memories of Father when she was young, of Mother, of growing up with Susannah—these were hers to keep. But returning to Chicago to run the boardinghouse? She had no desire to do it. It would mean going backward in time to a Sarah who no longer existed. Chicago was in her past, not her future.

"If you were to retain your property, it could provide a continuous, comfortable living for you. On the other hand, if you decided to sell it, the amount from the sale might mean a nice dowry for both you and your sister."

"Are you saying that in either case I would have to return to Chicago?"

"That is correct."

"But what if I didn't . . . couldn't?"

Mr. Vonachek looked stern. "Please take time to consider what I have told you."

Chapter 9

* * *

The other boarders began to gather in the parlor, and Sarah was thankful that her conversation with Mr. Vonachek was interrupted.

They were called to the dining room, where Susannah had set Sarah's usual place. But Sarah picked up her plate, napkin, and utensils and carried them into the kitchen, putting them on the kitchen table with the other two place settings.

"I didn't think you'd want to wait," Susannah told her. "There's no telling when Clint will get here."

Susannah's glance fell on the silver-and-garnet pin, and for a moment the set of her shoulders softened, but Sarah could see a trace of resentment in Susannah's eyes. She took her sister's hands and begged, "Don't be angry, Susannah. I already apologized, but if it will make you happy, I'll apologize again."

"I'm not angry." Susannah tried to tug her hands away.

"Then where's your smile?" Sarah teased. "Let's see a sweet smile!"

"Don't talk to me as though I were a child!" Susannah snapped, and in surprise Sarah let go of her hands.

"I didn't think I was."

"Well, you were."

"Then I apologize for that, too. Susannah . . ."

At that moment a cleaned-up, spruced-up Clint walked into the kitchen, saying, "Something smells mighty good."

Susannah perked up and ran to get his plate. With a radiant smile she said, "I promise you're going to like this."

"Since you did the cooking, I know I will," Clint answered, and Susannah giggled at his praise.

Sarah smiled at them both, relieved that Susannah's bad mood had passed. "Tell us about the trip up here," she said to Clint. "Were there any spills? Any bad problems with the weather?"

The three of them sat at one end of the kitchen table, but aside from praising Susannah's cooking and answering Sarah's questions about the ride from Denver to Leadville, Clint didn't do much talking. He ate ravenously, and his eyes on Sarah were every bit as hungry.

When Sarah jumped up to help Susannah clear the table and clean the kitchen, Clint did, too, the three of them working together; but when the dishes had been put away and there was nothing left for Susannah to do but set the table for the next morning's breakfast, Clint drew Sarah aside.

"Let her do the rest of her job alone," he said. "I think I found out something, and I want to tell you in private."

It was hard to find an unoccupied space downstairs, but Sarah remembered a small sewing room near the back stairs, and she led Clint there, closing the door behind them. It was crowded with some large packages of supplies, a cutting table, an overstuffed chair with a few worn places on the arm, and some bolts of fabric; but they squeezed inside, careful not to upset the papers of pins and pattern laid out on a piece of heavy, unbleached muslin.

Sarah placed the oil lamp on the table and eagerly asked, "What have you found out?"

"I said I *think* I might have found something," Clint amended. "I won't know until I ride up there."

Sarah tried to hide her impatience. "What is it?"

Clint frowned as he thought. "A run-down old cabin—an abandoned mine shack. It's high up on Pine Ridge above the route I take with the coach. I can see only a small part of it—mainly the chimney—through the pines."

"What's important about this cabin?"

"Smoke," Clint said. "It was coming from the chimney. Who'd stay in a run-down shack that nobody would want to live in, on a no-good mining claim that nobody in his right mind would work?"

Sarah suddenly understood. "Someone hiding out. Do you think it's Eli Wulfe?"

"Yes. That's exactly what I was thinking," Clint said, "and I'll know for sure when I go up there and find out."

"No!" Through Sarah's mind flashed a terrifying image of Eli hearing Clint coming, lying in wait for him, his gun ready. Trembling, she grabbed Clint's shoulders, holding him tightly. "This is a job for the marshal and a posse, not one person. Wulfe's a dangerous man."

"It might not be Wulfe who's up there."

"If it is, he'd hear you coming. He'd have the advantage, and against the snow you'd be a target." Her hands slid down to encircle him as though she could physically hold

93

him back. "Promise me you won't try to handle this yourself. I couldn't stand it if anything happened to you. Please . . . promise me!"

His arms were around her, his lips against her cheek. "If you care about me that much, Sarah, then I promise." He tucked his fingers under her chin and raised her face so that she was looking into his eyes. "About that other promise I made—" he began, but a knock at the door interrupted them.

They parted just before the door opened. "I saw light under the door," Mrs. Hannigan said, looking from Sarah to Clint and back again, her forehead wrinkling into a frown.

"Clint was telling me something relating to my father's murder," Sarah quickly explained. She tucked back a wisp of hair that had come loose and hoped Mrs. Hannigan wouldn't take note of the flush that warmed her cheeks. "We needed privacy, and I didn't think you'd mind if we spoke in your sewing room."

The frown disappeared, but Mrs. Hannigan said firmly, "The kitchen would have been a more suitable place for a young lady to speak with a gentleman friend."

"Susannah was in the kitchen."

"If there's information to be told about your father, don't you think she'd want to share it? He was her father, too."

"You're right, Mrs. Hannigan," Clint said. "And I take full blame. I sure wasn't thinking about rules and manners or about Susannah's part in all this. All I had on my mind was some information to give to Sarah, and I wanted to keep it private."

As Sarah picked up the oil lamp and they joined Mrs. Hannigan in the hall, the landlady's curiosity got the better of her. She leaned toward them and in a conspiratorial whisper asked, "You said the information relates to Ben Lindley's murder. Does that mean it has to do with Eli Wulfe's whereabouts?"

Clint looked toward Sarah for an answer, but Sarah had none. However, the silence was answer enough for Mrs. Hannigan. She went on, "I thought that terrible man would have traveled far from here by this time." She shuddered and glanced to each side as though Eli Wulfe might suddenly spring from one of the shadows. "If you know where he is, then go to the marshal . . . now. I can't believe that Sarah will be safe until Mr. Wulfe is locked up."

Sarah felt helpless. She shouldn't have given Mrs. Hannigan any kind of explanation. With the little she'd said, Mrs. Hannigan had come too close to the truth.

Clint lowered his voice. "I'll do as you say, ma'am, and I know I can trust you not to mention any part of our conversation."

"I won't speak a word of it!" Mrs. Hannigan pressed a hand to her heart.

"I'll go now, Sarah," Clint said. "It may take time to find Marshal Kelly."

Mrs. Hannigan sniffed. "Not if you start looking in the right places. From what I hear, he's often to be found in Owens' Faro Club."

"After you leave, I'll talk to Susannah about what you told me," Sarah said to Clint. "She's probably still in the kitchen."

"No, she's in the parlor." Mrs. Hannigan put a hand to her forehead. "My, oh, my! Our conversation drove all other thoughts out of my mind. I forgot to tell you, Sarah, that Mr. Jeremy Caulfield is here to see you. Susannah said she'd chat with him while I went to fetch you."

95

As Mrs. Hannigan took the lamp, Sarah caught a quick glimpse of Clint's scowl. Silently they followed Mrs. Hannigan toward the parlor.

Jeremy jumped to his feet as he saw Sarah, but there was no warmth in his greeting as he acknowledged Clint.

Susannah's expression was so vulnerable, so hurt, that no one could miss it. Sarah quickly put an arm around her sister and hugged her close, and Clint said, "Susannah, I didn't take your feelings into consideration, and I apologize. There was something I thought Sarah should know, and I guess I was just trying to spare you any worry."

"Well, we hope that none of us will need to worry after Clint talks to the marshal," Mrs. Hannigan said.

Jeremy's eyes narrowed as he studied Clint. "Worry about what?"

"None of your . . . Never mind," Clint answered.

Mrs. Hannigan gave Clint a nervous glance and said, "I promised not to speak a word of it, so let's discuss something else."

"Not just yet," Jeremy said. "If Clint's going to talk to the marshal, his conversation would most likely be in reference to a crime. If the crime had to do with a holdup or shooting, there'd be no need for secrecy. Also, the crime that would interest Clint the most would be the murder of Ben Lindley, and the only thing about the murder that could still worry Mrs. Hannigan and Ben Lindley's daughters would be the whereabouts of the murderer." He paused, glancing at Sarah and Mrs. Hannigan, as though looking for telltale expressions on their faces, before he added, "I'm guessing that Clint has discovered where Eli Wulfe is hiding."

Sarah knew she was staring with amazement, but so were the others.

Jeremy noted their expressions and said proudly, "I'm learning to think like a reporter."

Clint grumbled, "There's no need for you to puff up like an overfed sage hen. Mrs. Hannigan figured it out quicker than you did."

Ignoring the remark, Jeremy said, "You may as well tell us. Where is Eli Wulfe?"

Clint didn't answer. His eyebrows drew together, and his jaw stiffened.

"Good evening," a voice said in Sarah's ear, and she whirled to see Mr. Vonachek.

"Good evening," she said with enthusiasm, desperately grateful for the interruption. "Mr. Vonachek, have you met Mr. Barnes and Mr. Caulfield?"

"Yes, I have," he said, and shook hands with both men. "Do you mind if I join you?"

"Please do," Sarah said, and perched in the middle of the sofa. Jeremy immediately sat on one side of her, Clint on the other.

"I thought you mentioned having to leave us, Mr. Barnes," Mrs. Hannigan said, her eyebrows wiggling signals.

"Not just yet," Clint answered.

Susannah sat on a chair beside Clint, and Mr. Vonachek pulled up chairs for Mrs. Hannigan and himself.

"There now," Mrs. Hannigan said as she smoothed her skirt across her lap. "We've made a nice, conversational circle."

Oh, would that it were so! Sarah thought. She was well aware that Clint and Jeremy were glaring at each other over her head. Frantically searching for a topic of conversation, she turned to Mr. Vonachek. "Leadville is a long way from Philadelphia and must be a very different place in which to live. How did you happen to come here?"

97

"On my thirtieth birthday I found I had reached a point in my life in which I wanted to travel and try something new." Mr. Vonachek spoke easily, his features animated, as if he were pleased that someone would be interested in his life. "I enjoy the mountains, so I decided to accept a position with the city of Leadville. Fortunately I enjoy working with figures, and for the past two years I have found the growth of the area through property development and prospecting claims highly interesting."

He paused, as though waiting for questions, and when there were none, he politely turned to Clint and said, "Your job seems to be very interesting. It must require a great deal of skill, since on every trip you carry the lives of your passengers in your hands."

Clint squirmed, uncomfortable at being the center of attention. "It's a job," he mumbled.

"Clint told me he's been held up by masked gunmen, and once he even had to save his passengers from a starving band of wolves," Susannah murmured, her eyes shining. "He's very, very brave."

Clint turned a dark red, but Jeremy said, "Being brave is easy when there's plenty of company with you—all of them with guns."

"Maybe I should take on a job like yours," Clint told him, "where I dress like a dude and push a little pencil around on a piece of paper."

"You'd find it's much more difficult than you can imagine to turn your thoughts into words on paper," Jeremy said. "To begin with, of course, you need to have thoughts worth putting into words."

Sarah jumped to her feet. "I'm going to get my coat," she

said to Clint, "and go with you to see . . . go with you on your errand."

Sarah was aware that Mr. Vonachek was staring at them with surprise, but there was no way she could explain, and something had to be done to end Clint and Jeremy's argument.

Clint stood slowly. "I don't know where we'll find him, and I'm sure as h— . . . There are some places I'm not going to let you set foot in. Besides, I only brought the one horse."

"Then I can help." Jeremy got to his feet. "I came in Uncle's carriage, so Sarah can ride with me."

"What business is this of yours?" Clint demanded, but Sarah interrupted.

"There's room in the carriage for all three of us," she said. "We can try the office first."

Susannah stood. "I'll come, too."

Sarah answered Susannah more abruptly than she'd intended. "No. You may not."

As Susannah's face began to cloud with anger, Sarah softened the tone of her voice and said, "Please, Susannah. Where we're going is not a proper place for a young girl to be, and I would worry about you. I'd rather you remained at home with Mrs. Hannigan."

Their landlady quickly got up and put an arm around Susannah's shoulders, hugging her close. "Sarah is right," she said. "You'd be better off here with me."

"I'll tell you everything later," Clint said to her. "You have every right to know."

"You promise?"

"I promise."

Susannah's face cleared. "I want to hear all about it."

"I'm sure we all do," Mr. Vonachek said.

"Thank you, Susannah." Sarah gave her sister a quick hug, which Susannah refused to return.

"I'll be waiting" she said, looking past Sarah to Clint.

Chapter 10

♦ ♦ ♦

Clint, who seemed so much in command while riding Samson, looked awkward and out of place as the only passenger in the backseat of the Caulfields' carriage. In contrast, Jeremy drove with a practiced ease. Sarah wondered if she was being influenced by Susannah; she couldn't help keeping track of the differences between the two men.

Jeremy had grown up with fine carriages and expensive, matched pairs of horses; whereas Clint had gone through his growing years working long hours, and the only wheeled transportation he must have known as a boy would have been the jouncing, slow-moving farm wagons. For an instant she pictured a tangle of black curls over a serious—and probably dirty—small boy's face, and she smiled.

It was pretty obvious that Jeremy would continue to want and insist on only the best, but—as Susannah had pointed out—Clint's dream of building his own ranch involved a great deal more of the hard work he was used to. There was no question that Jeremy's standard of living would be decidedly more comfortable. Susannah would certainly count that in his favor.

Street traffic was once again heavy, as though the vigilantes' hangings had never taken place. Music blared from the gambling halls and saloons, and the cold night air was sour with the stench of horses and their droppings and of countless unwashed bodies.

Jeremy pulled the horses to a stop, jumped down from the carriage, and secured the reins to one of the hitching posts in the street in front of the marshal's office.

There were only a few people in the room besides the man behind a desk: a derelict asleep on a cot in one corner, and two men hunched in conversation next to the potbellied stove. They looked up out of curiosity, stared boldly at Sarah, and went back to their talk.

The man in charge introduced himself as Tom Spradley, the marshal's chief deputy, and told them that Marshal Kelly was down with the grippe. Spradley knew Jeremy and said, "If you're here to get a story for your newspaper, there's nothin' much that's happened, aside from the usual. They brought in a body found on the street in front of Miller's Saloon, but he weren't murdered, just froze to death."

"I didn't come for a story," Jeremy told him. "Mr. Barnes has something to tell you."

"All right. Let's hear it," Spradley said, and Clint related the information he'd given to Sarah.

Both the deputy and Jeremy listened intently, Spradley nodding as he recognized the mine shack in the location Clint described. "The old *Fidelity* mine," Spradley said.

"*Fidelity?* Isn't that one of the Caulfield mines?" Sarah asked in amazement.

102

Spradley nodded and said, "That Eli Wulfe's a bad one. It's gonna take some careful plannin' to flush him out."

"The sooner you go after him the better," Clint warned.

One of the men at the stove said, loud enough to be overheard, "There's plenty of decent folks in town needin' help. Don't make much sense to waste time goin' after the murderer of a murderer."

Sarah gasped. "My father was not a murderer!" she cried.

Clint took a threatening step toward the man, who took one look at Clint and quickly said, "Sorry, ma'am. Sorry. Didn't mean to speak outta turn."

"I'll notify the marshal, and we'll get some men together by midmornin' at least," Spradley said. "It'll take what . . . one hour?—two?—to ride there?"

"Closer to two," Clint said. "I'll be on hand. I'll show you the shortcut."

Sarah sucked in her breath, wishing Clint wouldn't go.

Sudden suspicion drew the deputy's eyes into a squint as he studied Clint's face. "You a member of that Merchants Protective Patrol?"

"No, and I had no part in the vigilantes' hangings."

"Makes no never mind," the deputy answered. "Considerin' how folks felt about what took place, we're drawin' a clear line between peace officers and the citizenry. Goin' after Eli Wulfe ain't the kind of action that calls for deputizin' men for a posse. We got enough duly sworn-in peace officers to handle it."

"But I know the fastest way to get there," Clint insisted.

"No matter. You leave this up to us."

Sarah let out a sigh of relief.

Clint frowned with impatience as he asked, "Will you let

us know if it is Wulfe up there and if you're able to arrest him?"

The deputy nodded. "Come by sometime midafternoon. We'll be back by then."

"Better yet," Jeremy said cheerfully, "I'll be setting type early tomorrow morning, so you can read my story in *The Leadville Daily Star.*"

"You keep this to yourself," Clint warned him. "The fewer people who know about it the better."

"My job is bringing news to the people of Leadville."

"But what I told Spradley is confidential."

"Not if it's news." Jeremy half closed his eyes and began to recite: "*An abandoned mine shack with its broken windows and door hanging loose on rusted hinges, battered by cold winds and drifts of snow . . . a run-down, deserted shack used as a refuge for small, helpless woodland creatures . . . Has this symbol of a prospector's mine that failed, of hopes and dreams that were crushed, become the hideout for a murderer, desperate to escape the hanging knot of justice?*"

Clint's large hands clenched into fists, but he kept them at his side. "I doubt if anybody could stand to read that drivel, but I'm not going to let you print anything that would tip off Eli Wulfe's friends that the law was coming after him."

"Friends?" Jeremy gave Clint a long, slow look, and Sarah could see the spark of mischief in his eyes as he continued reciting: "*A man without a friend in the world . . . a lonely, hunted gunman . . . Eli Wulfe lights a fire for warmth, and the telltale plume of smoke that rises from the chimney of the cabin betrays his whereabouts to the men intent on his capture.*"

Jeremy was deliberately baiting Clint. Even if Jeremy did write the story and set it into type, *The Star* wasn't due on the streets until early afternoon, long after the marshal's men would have left to find Eli.

But Clint didn't stop to think it out. He stepped forward and grabbed two fistfuls of Jeremy's coat. "Let's go outside and talk about this," he demanded.

"Clint!" Sarah cried. "Please let go of Jeremy. He can't put that story in the newspaper in time, and he knows it. He was just having fun teasing."

Clint didn't let go. "There's no reason for him to make fun at others' expense."

Jeremy didn't try to squirm loose. His eyes mirrored the light, mocking smile on his lips as he stared at Clint.

"Please, Clint!" Sarah grabbed his right arm and hung on until his hands opened and dropped to his side.

Jeremy straightened his clothing, brushing off his coat. He asked Clint, "If we gave each other sore jaws and black eyes, what would that prove?"

"I wasn't out to prove anything," Clint answered. "I was out to stop you from writing a story we'd all regret."

"Use your mind, if you can," Jeremy said. "There's a better way of reaching solutions than using your fists. *Words* can settle arguments better than violence."

To Sarah's surprise Clint slowly nodded. "Maybe you're right about that," he said, and slowly grinned. "All along you were probably counting on Sarah's words to save your hide."

Jeremy flushed, but Sarah stepped between Clint and Jeremy and took their arms. "Let's go, please," she said. "Susannah and Mrs. Hannigan will be worrying about us." She thanked Deputy Spradley and sailed from the office, Jeremy and Clint hurrying to catch up.

During the ride back to Mrs. Hannigan's, the antagonism

between the two men was so thick that Sarah finally lost her patience. As the carriage pulled up in front of the house, she put a hand on Jeremy's arm and said, "Thank you for taking us to the marshal's office. I appreciate your kindness, but I'm going to say good night to you right now."

His surprised glance immediately shifted to Clint, who had jumped from the carriage and stood ready to help Sarah down, but Sarah quickly added, "Clint is going to tell Susannah what the marshal's deputy said, and then he is going to leave, too. He put in a long, hard day's driving, and I know he's tired."

"I'm not tired," Clint said.

"Well, I am," Sarah told him. Frustrated with both Clint and Jeremy, she marched ahead of Clint into the house.

Susannah was waiting, and Sarah said, "We talked to a deputy marshal. Clint will tell you all about it."

She kissed Susannah's cheek, said good night to both Susannah and Clint, and went up the stairs without glancing back.

While Sarah got ready for bed, she expected Susannah to join her soon, wanting to talk about what had taken place. But as she scooted under the quilts, shivering a little as she waited to get warm, Susannah still hadn't come. It was much later that Sarah roused from sleep enough to know that Susannah had slipped into bed beside her.

In the morning Sarah was thankful to find that Susannah's mood had changed and she was once again cheerful. Although it was Saturday and there would be no classes, Sarah rose early and lent her sister a hand in preparing breakfast.

Sarah had given a great deal of thought to the antagonism

between Clint and Jeremy and had begun to worry that Jeremy might want to irritate Clint even further by actually printing that story about the search for Eli Wulfe.

Jeremy had said that he'd have to set type that morning. Very well, then. She'd show up at the office of *The Leadville Daily Star* and make sure there would be no story about Eli.

When she arrived at the office, Jeremy already stood at the bulky Washington handpress. Wrapped in a large, ink-stained apron, he was busy laying a sheet of paper on the inked form, cranking the carriage into place, then lowering the platen to make the ink impression.

Chester Caulfield was not in sight, so Sarah merely smiled at two men, who looked up from their desks as she passed, and made her way to Jeremy's side. Papers and books cluttered the desks and tables, cartons lined the walls, and the slightly bitter, pungent smell of wet ink filled the room.

As Sarah approached, Jeremy raised the platen, rolled back the carriage, removed the printed sheet, and began the process again.

"Jeremy," Sarah said.

He looked up with surprise but didn't stop working. "What is it, Sarah?" Jeremy asked, lowering the platen onto the next page.

"I'm sorry everyone was so out of sorts last night," she said. "I—I wanted to talk to you about what you said."

Without breaking the rhythm of his work, Jeremy looked up and grinned. "I said quite a bit. Was it any particular remark? Maybe the one about Clint being particularly suited to raising dumb animals?"

"Don't start that again," Sarah said firmly. "You're being unfair. Clint is one of the most intelligent men I know." She wished she didn't have to talk to Jeremy with the clatter and clank of the handpress between them. "I want to make sure that *The Star* isn't going to include a story about the peace officers going after Eli Wulfe."

Jeremy raised the platen and pulled a printed sheet from the press, handing it to Sarah. "There's no story about Eli in *The Star*," he said. "Here's the front page. You can read it for yourself. Just watch out for the ink. It's still wet and could get on your clothes."

Sarah held the sheet out to the side, not looking at it. "If you say the story's not in it, I believe you," she told him.

An older man, also covered with an apron, stepped to Jeremy's side and said, "I'll take over here for a while. You go talk to your lady friend."

"Thanks," Jeremy told him. He wiped the ink from his hands on a rag that smelled of kerosene, took the sheet from Sarah, and walked with her toward the front of the large, cluttered room. It was quiet here, yet out of the hearing of the men at the desks.

Sarah held out a hand toward the doorknob, but Jeremy put a hand over hers, pulling it back. "Don't go," he said. "And don't be angry with me, Sarah. If you want me to apologize, I will." He gave a rueful smile. "When I saw that cowboy with you last night, I was jealous."

"You and I are friends, Jeremy," Sarah began, but Jeremy interrupted.

"The way I feel about you is much more than friendship," he said. "Can't you see, Sarah? We were brought together for a purpose."

"Don't, Jeremy," Sarah said, but Jeremy persisted.

"You could have left Leadville, but you stayed. You even sent for your sister. I've been hoping you made that decision because of me." When she didn't answer, he asked, "Was I wrong, Sarah?"

Had her feelings for Jeremy influenced her decision to stay? Sarah tried to be truthful with herself, but she honestly didn't know.

One of the men in the room had left his work and was staring at her. Sarah hoped he couldn't overhear what they were saying.

"Come outside," Sarah murmured to Jeremy. "Just for a minute."

He snatched a heavy coat from the rack by the door, pulled it on, and followed her out to the sidewalk. Sarah hesitated. From the moment she'd met Jeremy, she'd felt close to him. She'd confided in him before, and she had wanted to—had even tried to—at the dance, but Jeremy had not been interested then in her story of promises and responsibility. Now, since there was danger in knowing, it seemed wrong to bring Jeremy into it.

"I told you about my promise to Father," she said.

He nodded impatiently. "I remember."

"There's much more to it than I told you," she said, looking up at him. "When the time comes, I'll tell you the rest, but I can't tell you now. You'll have to trust me."

He gripped her shoulders and bent his head, almost touching her own. "Why can't *you* trust *me?*"

"I do!" she cried, tears blurring her vision as she realized that she was hurting Jeremy. "All I'm asking you to do is be patient with me. Give me the chance to work out my problems and try to make the right decisions."

Jeremy released his grip. "All right, Sarah," he said. "I'll do whatever will please you."

Her smile wobbled as she said, "Thank you. And thank you for not writing a story about Eli."

"When they catch and arrest him, I will."

"Then it will be all right."

"With the cowboy, I suppose."

"No, with me."

"I've got to get back to work," Jeremy said. "When can I see you again?"

"Not for a while," Sarah said. "I need some time."

It was true, and she hoped that Jeremy would understand and accept her excuse. But she had another reason for not wanting to see Jeremy for a few days. Sarah was sure Clint would come calling tonight. She certainly didn't want to be in the middle of another skirmish between Clint and Jeremy. It would be much better to keep them apart.

As soon as Sarah returned to Mrs. Hannigan's, she went upstairs and worked, preparing her classroom lessons for the following week at the little desk in her room; but she kept her door ajar, eagerly listening for the opening of the front door and Clint's deep voice.

By the noon meal Clint still hadn't come. Fearing that she had been too brusque with him the night before and regretting it, Sarah went downstairs, where she chose to eat in the kitchen with her sister.

As they ate, Susannah happily chatted on about some gossip Mr. Vonachek had told her, and Sarah smiled.

"I knew you'd think that was funny," Susannah said.

"It wasn't Mr. Vonachek's story that made me smile," Sarah answered. "I was smiling because of you. I love seeing you so happy, and I'm glad we're friends again."

Sarah was shocked by the sudden, stricken look that flashed across Susannah's face. It was replaced so quickly by a bland, nondescript expression, that Sarah wondered if she'd only imagined it. "Susannah?" she asked. "Is something wrong?"

"Nothing's wrong," Susannah said. She jumped to her feet and took their plates from the table, leaving Sarah bewildered. Susannah was covering up something she didn't want Sarah to know.

There was nothing Sarah could do about it now. She heard the boarders leaving the dining room, so she set to work clearing the table.

"You don't have to help me," Susannah said.

"I'm glad to," Sarah told her. "I want a chance to talk with you."

There was a quick glance of resentment. "To tell me what to do?"

"No, of course not. I thought you might like to discuss what Clint told you."

The rigid line left Susannah's shoulders, and her voice softened. "There isn't much to talk about. He told me what the deputy marshal said. I'm glad they're going after Eli. I hope they catch him."

"Clint wanted to go with the peace officers. I'm glad Deputy Spradley refused to give him permission."

Susannah, who'd been pouring boiling water into the dishwashing pan, put down the kettle and stared at Sarah. "Clint told me they needed him to show them the fastest route."

"Oh, no!" Sarah cried, shaken with a desperate fear. "He shouldn't have gone! Why does he insist on putting his life in danger?"

"But he hasn't, has he?" Susannah began to look frightened. "Clint told me not to worry. He said he'd be riding

111

with a group of peace officers, and they'd take Eli Wulfe by surprise, and it would be over before anyone knew what happened."

Sarah gripped the edge of the table. "Susannah, you think you're an adult, but do you see how young you really are? You believed that? Didn't it occur to you that Eli isn't going to give up willingly? He's armed, and he's a murderer, and he knows he could be tried and hanged."

"Oh." Susannah's face drained of color, and tears came to her eyes. "I should have tried to talk Clint out of going. I didn't understand." With a flash of anger, she cried, "Why didn't you tell me all this last night instead of running off the way you did?"

"It's not fair to blame me, Susannah," Sarah told her. "I left because I—I didn't want to talk to Clint any longer."

But Susannah wasn't listening to her. As her concern grew, so did her anger. "You didn't care what happened to him," she cried.

"I did! I do!"

"Why don't you just marry Jeremy so that Clint will stop thinking about you and can marry someone who'd be right for him? You're not. He needs a down-to-earth wife who can work beside him, not a dreamer who holds to useless promises!"

Sarah didn't answer, and she didn't try to soothe her sister, who turned away from her, leaning against the drain board as she sobbed.

Susannah was in love with Clint! Sarah tried to understand. How could she have missed what was happening? Her feelings were in a muddle as resentment—even a little anger—seeped in. Clint had been calling on *her*—Sarah. How dare Susannah try to take him away!

She wasn't being fair. She'd put her promise to Father above all else and refused to consider her feelings for Clint and Jeremy.

Her heart aching, Sarah realized she had made a choice, and it wasn't logical or even carefully thought out. The moment she knew Clint's life was in danger and she could lose him, she knew she couldn't exist without him.

And now, Susannah . . .

Sarah was vaguely aware that hurried, heavy footsteps were pounding across the dining room, but she was startled when the kitchen door flew open and Clint stomped into the room.

He didn't even look at Susannah. His eyes were on Sarah, the anger in them like blue sparks.

"That swell who works on his uncle's newspaper," Clint snapped. "What was he telling you this morning, Sarah?"

Clint had seen her with Jeremy? Then why hadn't he made himself known? Sarah stammered, "H-he r-reassured me that he hadn't written a story about the marshal's men looking for Eli Wulfe."

"He didn't need to," Clint said. "By the time we got to the mine shack, all we found was a fire in the fireplace and a half-eaten meal. Eli Wulfe cleared out in a hurry, because someone tipped him off that we were coming!"

Chapter 11

◆　◆　◆

Sarah backed into a chair. "Clint!" she cried. "Surely you don't think that Jeremy sent word to Eli Wulfe!"

"Who else would?"

"Why . . . why . . . anyone in the marshal's office could have. Anyone who learned about the cabin."

"Like Susannah or Mrs. Hannigan?"

Sarah felt her cheeks burn. She got to her feet, aware that Susannah had composed herself and was watching this exchange intently. "Please, Clint," Sarah said, "be reasonable. Jeremy is a friend. He's been kind and helpful, and I know he wouldn't do anything to warn Eli to get away."

"*You* be reasonable!" he demanded. "I told you what I suspect about Caulfield, and you didn't even take time to consider it. Right away you started defending him."

What Clint said was true, which made Sarah even more upset. "You accused him without proof!"

"If proof's what you want, I'll get the proof."

"No!" Sarah cried. "Leave Jeremy alone!"

Clint was suddenly silent. His shoulders sagged, and he

leaned against the wall, his anger spent, the expression on his face one of defeat. "All right, Sarah," he said. "If that's the way you want it."

She took a step toward him, her hands held out, but he didn't respond. "Please try to understand," she said.

"I'm afraid I do," he told her.

"No," Sarah said. "No, you don't."

But Clint abruptly turned and stalked out of the kitchen. Without a word Susannah ran after him.

Sarah, her eyes burning painfully with tears she forced back, ducked through the back hallway in order to avoid the parlor and ran upstairs.

She flopped down on the bed and cried until no more tears came. She had tried to make her own decisions, to take charge of her life and to guide Susannah's, but everything had gone wrong. She had only succeeded in hurting the three people who meant the most to her. She had thought she had changed, had grown up, but now all her old doubts rushed back to torment her.

As she sat up, her glance fell on the photograph of her mother, and she reached for it, hugging it to her chest. "Oh, Mother, help me!" she murmured. "What am I going to do?"

Into her mind came the last words her father had spoken, the words which had seemed so puzzling: "Remember . . . your mother . . . Margaret."

Sarah held the photograph in her lap and studied it. As Father was dying, he had spoken about proof of wrongdoing and had been trying so hard to tell her something about it. What did Mother have to do with the proof Father had hidden?

Her excitement growing, she turned the silver frame over

and gently slid out the velvet-covered board that held the photograph in place. There it was! Sarah extracted a thin, folded sheet of paper that had been tucked between the back of the photograph and the board.

As Sarah lay the pieces of the picture frame on the bed beside her and opened the sheet of paper, her fingers shook so much that the paper rustled.

In small, firm script at the top of the paper, she read three names: Wilbur Owens, Homer Morton, Chester Caulfield. Sarah gasped. Homer Morton was the banker she'd met on the stagecoach ride to Leadville, and—although it took a moment to place his name—Sarah remembered the short, rude man she'd met at the Texas House. Bessie, who'd worked there as a waitress, had told her who he was: Wilbur Owens, the man who owned Owens' Faro Club. However, the name that stunned her was Chester Caulfield's. Jeremy's uncle!

What followed was a brief account, written in a type of shorthand, but Sarah could follow it:

Caulfield set up syndicate aftr reptr (Harry Lewis) uncovered Morton's scheme to skim accts. Blackmail first, but not enough for Caulfield. Owens reprts prospctrs with plenty spnd money. Sees pattrn. Knows which areas are real prdcrs. Morton solicits for mine expansion, offr loans. Arrngd so syndicate gets large share. Then bank skims each month. Syndicate prosprs two ways.

Next came two mysterious columns of letters, most of them in pairs, with numbers following: *SG*—60,000; *DL*—90,000; *F*—45,000; *CH*—50,000; *L*—75,000. There were ten groups in the first list, twelve in the second, and they looked almost like the tidy columns of daily accounts kept by a butcher or greengrocer. But these lists of Father's meant nothing to Sarah, and for the moment what she had already read gave her enough to think about.

Apparently Jeremy's uncle had discovered, through one of his reporters, that Homer Morton was stealing money from the bank accounts of the miners. How had Morton managed to get away with this? Very probably most of the men would trust the bank to take care of their money and wouldn't question the amounts in their accounts. It was also likely that many of them who came from the European and Slavic countries couldn't read or knew only a little English and would therefore be unable to check easily on the banker's actions.

Blackmail not enough, Father had written. With a shudder of distaste for the duplicity and greed of Chester Caulfield, Sarah thought about the scheme he had masterminded. Wilbur Owens would be in a good position to see which miners were coming to his gaming house with ready money. Then he'd be able to get information about the locations of the mines these prospectors were working. If an area was producing well, Morton would offer a loan from his bank for expansion so the miner could do even better. Prospectors who were cautious might question and refuse the loans, but many of the miners were rough, uneducated men, and they wouldn't suspect that someone was taking advantage of them.

How had Father learned all this? Had he begun to suspect what was going on while he played cards at Owens' Faro Club?

Father had called this information his insurance policy. Had he meant that his knowledge would ensure his safety? Or had he been using it to ensure his livelihood? Sarah winced, forced to face the fact that her father had used the information for his own gain.

Bessie had said that Ezekiel Wulfe had seemed bent on picking a fight, as though he were looking for a chance to shoot Ben Lindley. *Of course, he was,* Sarah thought. *That's exactly what Morton, Owens, and Caulfield had hired him to do!*

Sarah put the picture frame together again and placed it back on the table, but she folded the piece of paper and held it securely in the palm of her left hand. Her throat was tight and her chest hurt as scenes flashed through her mind. Chester Caulfield's pretense of friendship . . . his questions . . . Mrs. Morton's interrogation . . . Now Sarah understood how Eli Wulfe had found Father. Jeremy knew where he was going, and he must have repeated the information to his uncle. Jeremy also had known that they'd discovered Eli's hiding place.

"Oh, Jeremy," she whispered, so hurt that she felt ill. "I trusted you, and now there's so much I don't understand. Did you know what your uncle would do with that information? Was Clint right about you?"

There was a light knock at the door, and Sarah heard Susannah call, "Sarah? May I come in?"

"Of course," Sarah answered, and as Susannah entered, Sarah said, "This is your room, too. You didn't have to knock."

Susannah's eyes were red, and the corners of her lips turned down. "I—I wasn't sure you'd want to talk to me."

"Of course I do," Sarah told her, a rush of pity for Susannah's misery sweeping over her. She held out a hand. "Here. Sit down with me."

"Clint didn't want to talk to me," Susannah murmured as

119

she perched next to Sarah. "I tried to get him to stay, but he wouldn't. He was in a terrible mood . . . because of you." She looked into Sarah's eyes and pleaded, "You could love Jeremy just as easily as Clint! And if you were spoken for, Clint might notice me! Sarah! I want him!"

Choosing her words carefully, Sarah said, "We can't hand Clint back and forth. Clint will make any decisions about his feelings himself."

Susannah's breath was uneven, and she sat stiffly, her hands clenched in her lap. "No matter what you say or do, I'm going to help him decide."

There was nothing Sarah could tell Susannah. Aching both for her sister and herself, she murmured, "I'm afraid I've already lost Clint. You don't have to think of me as competition."

Susannah surprised Sarah by asking, "Do you care very much?"

"Yes," Sarah said. "It hurts terribly." She could feel tears rising again, so she unfolded the sheet of paper and held it out. "Let's not talk about Clint. I have something very important to show you."

"What is this?" Susannah asked.

"The proof Father spoke about. It was hidden inside the frame that holds Mother's photograph."

"So that's what he meant!"

"Read it," Sarah told her.

As Susannah did, Sarah heard her sharp intake of breath, but she finished reading before she said, "Jeremy's uncle arranged it all. Does that mean Jeremy's in it, too?"

"He can't be."

"You *are* stubborn about him . . . just as Clint said."

"Don't you see, Susannah, that Jeremy would have no

reason to doubt the honor of his own uncle? We didn't suspect Mr. Caulfield, and Jeremy doesn't either."

Susannah didn't answer. She studied the paper and asked, "What are all these letters and numbers?"

"I don't know," Sarah said.

Susannah handed back the paper. "Well, then, you won't be able to do anything about this."

"What do you mean?" Sarah asked. "This is the proof. Father has written about the crime those three men are involved in."

"It's not proof. No matter what he wrote, it's only his word against theirs. As usual, Father wasn't being practical."

"But . . . but we could get proof. Someone could go over the bank accounts and the loan contracts."

Susannah got up and smoothed down her skirt. "Who?" she asked. "Do you think Mr. Morton is going to make those records available to you, or that Mr. Caulfield will tell you the name of the syndicate and how he set it up? Be realistic, Sarah. Those men are powerful. You haven't got a chance against them."

Sarah grasped frantically for a solution. "Father mentioned Pinkerton's Detective Agency. I'll send this proof to them."

"What will they do with it? No more than we could. And how could we pay them? Mr. Vonachek said they're a private agency for hire, not a law-enforcement agency."

"What Father told me and what I told you must be kept secret!" Sarah exclaimed. "Why did you tell Mr. Vonachek?"

"I didn't tell him a thing! Mr. Vonachek just happened to be discoursing about the Pinkerton's agency and how the railroads hired them to try to stop the train robberies."

Sarah grumbled, "Does Mr. Vonachek know *everything?*"

"Just about," Susannah said. "He's quite remarkable."

"Forget Mr. Vonachek. We're discussing the information on this paper."

"Not anymore, we aren't," Susannah said. "There's nothing left to discuss. Forget it, Sarah, and get on with your life."

"No," Sarah said. "I'm not going to give up, and it's not just because of the promise I made to Father. What these men are doing is a crime, and they must be stopped." She glanced down at the paper, the mysterious notations of letters and numbers jumping and squiggling before her eyes. "Maybe the proof is hidden somewhere in this code of letters and numbers."

"Well, I don't agree with you," Susannah told her. "No matter what you find, who's going to believe you and bring those men to justice? No one!"

She took a step closer to Sarah and lowered her voice. "There's something else you have to think about—something even more important. Look at me, Sarah."

Sarah looked up into Susannah's eyes, startled at the fear in her sister's face. "Think hard about what I'm telling you," Susannah said. "If Father was killed because of what he knew, and if his friend, Mrs. Fitch, was killed because someone thought she might have that paper you found, then think about what those people might do to you if they knew you had it. Oh, Sarah, destroy that stupid piece of paper! Burn it! Don't you realize? They'll want to kill you, too!"

Chapter 12

•   •   •

Sarah knew of the great danger, but she couldn't disregard the importance of what she had promised. Her answers to Susannah were noncommittal, and as soon as Susannah had left the room, Sarah reread her father's words.

Suddenly an idea brought her to her feet. Harry Lewis, the reporter, had uncovered the original information about wrongdoings at Mr. Morton's bank, yet Father had left Mr. Lewis out of his account from that point on. Was this because the reporter had no knowledge that the syndicate existed?

Perhaps Mr. Lewis would help her. But Sarah didn't know how to go about talking with him. She couldn't very well march into the offices of *The Leadville Daily Star* and ask to see Harry Lewis. What if Chester Caulfield was there? Sarah shuddered. If she saw Mr. Caulfield, she'd never be able to hide the loathing she now felt for him. He'd see it in her eyes, and he'd know that she'd uncovered his crime.

She would have to arrange a casual meeting with Jeremy— perhaps on the street—and ask him to introduce her to

Harry Lewis. *The Star* would soon be printed and ready for delivery, and Jeremy would leave the newspaper office. If she hurried, she might arrange what would look like an accidental meeting.

She was not worried about asking Jeremy for help. Clint had to be wrong about him. Hadn't Jeremy done everything he could do for her every step of the way from Chicago to her arrival in Leadville? Sarah refused to believe that Jeremy could be involved in anything that would put her life in danger.

Sarah opened a desk drawer, ready to tuck Father's sheet of paper inside, then had second thoughts. This paper was too important to leave anywhere it might be found.

Smiling as the solution came to her, Sarah stood and unbuttoned her dress. She loosened her corset just enough so that she could tuck the paper inside, tugged the strings to tighten it, and dressed herself again. Satisfied, she bundled up for her trip outside and left the house.

As she neared the block in which the newspaper office was located, Sarah saw Jeremy leave the building, and she ran to catch up with him, calling, "Jeremy!" and hoping she could be heard over the din of the wagon wheels and the shouts of the ore haulers and freighters.

He wheeled around, a smile brightening his face. As he hurried to join her, he asked, "Sarah? You came to see me?"

Sarah couldn't go through with the subterfuge of pretending to be merely passing by. "There's a reporter named Harry Lewis who works for your uncle's newspaper," she said. "I'd like to ask him a question. Will you introduce us?"

Jeremy looked puzzled. "No one by that name works for *The Star*."

"But he must!" Sarah blurted out.

124

One of the men she had seen working at a desk in the office of *The Star* came through the door, clutching his coat around his neck, his head down as though he were ramming it against the cold.

As he came abreast of them, Jeremy said, "Here's someone who might help you. Luther Dotson's been with *The Star* from the start."

"No, Jeremy." Sarah tugged at his sleeve.

Either Jeremy hadn't heard her, or he hadn't noticed the urgency in her voice. "Luther!" he called. "Stop a moment. Could you answer a question for us?"

"It's not important," Sarah said, but again Jeremy—intent on filling Sarah's request—paid no attention.

Dotson joined them, and Jeremy performed the introductions while Sarah squirmed.

"Mr. Dotson," she said, "it's much too cold to stand out here talking. My question isn't important. It can wait."

"It won't take long to ask," Jeremy offered good-naturedly. He turned to Luther Dotson. "Have you ever heard of anyone named Harry Lewis?"

"Harry? Yes. He used to work for *The Star*," Mr. Dotson answered. His wary glance jumped from Jeremy to Sarah and back again. "Why do you want to know about him?"

"Miss Lindley has something to ask him. Where is Lewis now?"

"What does it matter?"

"Because Miss Lindley wants to know, it matters," Jeremy said firmly.

Mr. Dotson narrowed his eyes and mumbled, "Last spring— April, I think, or was it May?—Harry got himself killed."

Sarah shivered. "How?" she asked.

Hunching himself even deeper into his coat collar, he

said, "Harry was a good reporter but never could hold his liquor. He got shot in a brawl at Owens' Faro Club."

Sarah struggled to keep her shock from showing in her eyes. "Who shot him?" she asked.

Mr. Dotson edged a little farther away. He peered out from under his coat collar and rapidly recited, as though he had memorized the answer, "Too many people were involved in the fight, and no one admitted to witnessing the shooting, so no one was charged."

Horrified, Sarah thought how easy it could have been to commit murder by involving Mr. Lewis in a fight and ending his life under the cover of the brawl. It was as devious a plan as the one that had been arranged for Father.

She wondered if Harry Lewis had told anyone else, aside from Chester Caulfield, what he'd found out about Mr. Morton's illegal way of conducting his banking business. He might well have discussed the information with someone else at work—perhaps someone like Luther Dotson. It was obvious that Mr. Dotson was unwilling to talk about Harry Lewis. Because he knew why Mr. Lewis had been killed? Or was there another reason? Sarah wondered just how loyal Mr. Dotson was to his employer.

Luther Dotson began to edge away, obviously eager to escape the questioning, but Jeremy said, "Don't rush off, Luther." He turned to Sarah and said, "Luther may know the answer to whatever it is you wanted to ask Harry Lewis."

Panic-stricken, Sarah stammered, "No, please. It isn't important. Please feel free to leave, Mr. Dotson. I'm sorry to have kept you out here in the cold."

Mr. Dotson gave her a long, hard look before he scuttled away, and Sarah couldn't help wondering what he was thinking.

Jeremy studied Sarah, a quizzical look in his eyes. "What's this all about, Sarah?" he asked. "What was your reason for wanting to talk to Harry Lewis?"

Sarah took a deep breath. "He knew my father, and there was something I wanted to ask him that had to do with Father's death. But now the question doesn't matter, because it can't be answered."

"Is it something I can help you with?"

"No, Jeremy."

"If there's ever anything I can do for you, please don't hesitate to ask me."

Sarah put a gloved hand on Jeremy's arm, and he scooped it into his own, holding it snugly. "You've helped me in so many ways, and I'm grateful, Jeremy," Sarah said. "There *is* a favor I want to ask of you. Please don't tell anyone that I was asking about Harry Lewis."

"Anyone?" His eyes became more searching. "You have someone in particular in mind, don't you?"

Why did her face so easily mirror her feelings? Sarah looked away, willing herself to keep from exposing her thoughts. It would be too painful to tell Jeremy what she knew about his uncle, and for that matter, why should he believe her?

When she hesitated, not answering, Jeremy asked, "What are you hiding? What are you keeping from me, Sarah?"

Why not tell Jeremy everything? she thought. *Why not tell him now?*

Sarah's attention was caught by someone else leaving *The Star*—Chester Caulfield! Fortunately his back was to her as he tugged the door closed.

It would be impossible to meet him and talk to him. Especially right now. "I must go," she murmured to Jeremy. Without a word of explanation, she turned and hurried across the street, picking her way carefully. She hoped with all her heart that Jeremy would do as she had requested, but she couldn't help worrying that she might have made a terrible mistake.

On the way home Sarah went over and over in her mind the lists of letters and numbers that were written on the sheet of paper. Ten on the left side, twelve on the right. Was it possible that the letters stood for the initials of people from whom the syndicate had stolen? Most notations used two letters in combination together, but some used only one, and one letter couldn't stand for a person's name. Everyone had at least two names.

However, the idea was worth exploring. She could visit the courthouse and try to match each pair of initials with names in the Leadville directory. It would be a long and tedious task, but it would be a start. The courthouse would be closed on Saturday afternoon, but perhaps she could visit it after school let out on Monday.

As Sarah entered Mrs. Hannigan's parlor, removing her boots and coat, Mr. Vonachek rose from the overstuffed chair where he was reading and gave her a cheerful greeting. "We have at least an hour before supper, Miss Lindley. Do you have time now for our talk about your property?" he asked.

"Oh, dear . . . no," Sarah said as she hurried toward the stairs. "Not at the moment, Mr. Vonachek. There's something I must do. Please excuse me."

She dashed up the stairs, refusing to feel guilty at the disappointed expression on Mr. Vonachek's face. At the moment she had no time to think about property rights in Chicago.

Sarah removed the sheet of paper from inside her corset,

128

copied only the letters and numbers onto another sheet of paper—in two rows, exactly as Father had written them—and tucked the original back into its snug place next to her body. The copied list she placed inside the poetry book and—afraid to leave it untended in her room—she carried it downstairs.

As she returned to the parlor, Mr. Vonachek popped out of his chair, a hopeful look on his face. "Have you found time for our discussion after all?" he asked.

"Not right now," Sarah began.

"What is it you're reading?" he asked pleasantly, and somehow managed to take the poetry book from her hands.

As Sarah clumsily tried to retrieve the book, it fell, the sheet of paper spilling out.

"I'm so sorry. Allow me," Mr. Vonachek said, and quickly bent to pick up the paper and the book. Before he handed back the paper, he glanced at it.

Sarah could see the curiosity on his face. She kept herself from snatching the paper from him and gently, but firmly, slid it from his fingers. "It's nothing," she said.

"A word game perhaps?"

"Perhaps," Sarah answered.

"A curious list," he said, and took the paper back. He opened it and studied it, while Sarah tried to convince herself that it didn't matter. She'd have nothing to fear from Mr. Vonachek.

He suddenly startled Sarah by saying, "The numerical notations are written in such large amounts, I assume they refer to some sort of financial transaction. Am I right?"

"I don't know," Sarah answered.

A pleased look came over his face. "Ah, so you must find the key? Well, I shall be most happy to help you."

"This list," Sarah began. "I must ask you to keep it confidential. It's very important that no one . . ."

He interrupted as though he hadn't heard a word of what she'd been saying. "My work involves supervising the listing of town property and filing of mining claims," he told her. "These letters seem to correspond to the mines without exception." He ran his finger down part of the first list and recited, "SG—the *South Gulch* . . . DL—the *Dixie Lady* . . . F—*Faretheewell* . . . CH—*Charlie's Hill* . . . L—*Luckylou.*"

"Oh!" Sarah gasped. "The mines! So that's it!"

Proudly beaming at Sarah, Mr. Vonachek said, "You see how it fits?" He pulled a pencil from his pocket as he asked, "Would you like me to write down the names?"

"Oh, please do!" Sarah clasped her hands together under her chin.

This information was the key to the proof she needed. It was no longer simply Father's word against the syndicate set up by Mr. Caulfield. With the names of the mines in hand, Sarah could talk to the prospectors who owned them and verify the loans. She hoped they had copies of their contracts with the bank. She needed to see them in order to know how and in what ways the syndicate was benefiting and if this information could be used against Caulfield, Morton, and Owens. "Mr. Vonachek," she impulsively blurted out, "could you tell me where I might find these mines?"

"Yes," he said, and pulled a pencil from his inside coat pocket. "Here . . . I'll draw a little map on the back of your paper.

"Now that I have answered your question," Mr. Vonachek said, "may I ask where you obtained this list and for what purpose?"

Sarah hesitated. "I wish I could tell you, but I can't. The

130

list must remain secret for the moment. As soon as I have all the information for which I'm searching, I'll inform you of everything."

At first he looked at her speculatively, one eyebrow twitching, but his delight in intrigue took over, and his eyes began to shine.

He handed Sarah the sheet of paper, but as she began to rise, he quickly said, "Miss Lindley, can you spare just a moment to listen to what I have to say about your property in Chicago?"

Sarah sat back on the sofa. After the favor Mr. Von-achek had done for her, the least she could do would be to listen politely to his suggestions. At the moment, though, she couldn't have been less interested in their Chicago boardinghouse.

"Now then," he said, settling himself with a wiggle into his chair, "we must begin with a discussion of property rights. Until you or your sister are married, your aunt and uncle can claim, rightfully or wrongfully, that they are your legal guardians."

Mr. Vonachek went on, but Sarah didn't listen. She nodded, she murmured, but eventually she couldn't stand it another second. She had to end this conversation. She stood, clutching the sheet of paper in her hand, and tried to keep the irritation from her voice as she said, "Thank you for your good advice, Mr. Vonachek."

"I trust you will give it some serious thought?"

"Yes," she answered. "And once again may I please request that you not mention the information I showed you to anyone? It *must* be kept secret."

"Never fear," he said, but Sarah could see the snap of interest in his eyes.

Desperately she realized that she couldn't have solved this puzzle alone. In asking for help she had given Jeremy and Mr. Dotson one piece of the puzzle, and now Mr. Vonachek had taken another. But what else could she do? She hurried out of the parlor, troubled by the curiosity and speculation on Mr. Vonachek's face.

As she returned to her room, she made a decision not to share with Susannah the information Mr. Vonachek had uncovered in Father's list. Too many people knew something about what Sarah was doing, and it might be safer for Susannah if she was kept unaware.

With a sigh Sarah tucked the sheet with the penciled-in names of mines into her drawstring purse and began to plan. Her next step would be to go to the mines and talk to their owners in order to complete the information she needed. Tomorrow afternoon she would borrow Lady for transportation. She didn't think Clint would mind. He had told her to feel free to use Lady at any time.

Oh, how she missed Clint! She wished she could tell him what she had learned and ask him to go with her to the mines, but under the circumstances she couldn't. It was a task she would have to do alone.

In an effort to put her problems out of her mind, Sarah helped Susannah and Mrs. Hannigan with supper preparations and later joined two other boarders in a game of jackstraws. It was a miserable evening. She had told Jeremy to stay away, and Clint had left her of his own volition. Sarah carefully balanced one thin jackstraw with another, flipping it out of the way, as she tried to ignore the terrible pain of her loneliness.

Chapter 13

◆　◆　◆

It was after church services when Sarah, Susannah, and Mrs. Hannigan returned to the house. Sarah immediately began searching at the bottom of the wardrobe for comfortable house shoes to replace the boots she was wearing, while Susannah changed from a pretty plum-colored wool dress into a blouse and skirt more suitable for helping to prepare and serve the noon meal.

Susannah paused, one hand on the top dresser drawer, and asked, "Sarah, were you looking for something in here?"

"Of course not." Sarah emerged from the wardrobe, shoes in hand. "That drawer is yours, and I respect your privacy."

"Someone was in it," Susannah said. "Look! My stockings and chemises are all in a muddle."

Sarah jumped up and stared into the drawer. "Who would have done that?" She immediately pulled out the other drawers in the dresser and discovered that the contents of all of them had been disturbed.

"I don't understand it," Susannah said. "All the boarders were at church services. No one was here."

"Except the person who did this," Sarah said. She quickly glanced at the bedside table. Mother's photograph was lying facedown, the backing to the frame shoved in at an awkward angle. Her heart fluttered as she realized how close she had come to losing the paper that had been hidden there, and she plopped down on the bed.

As Sarah's foot brushed something, she bent to pick it up. It was Father's book of poems, its pages bent and its cloth cover ripped apart. Sarah tried to smooth the pages, then cradled the treasured book to her chest, her eyes filling with tears.

"Someone must have been searching for the paper Father left. Look what they did to his book!"

"Oh, Sarah," Susannah murmured as she bent to hug her sister. "Don't cry. I can repair the book. With a pretty piece of fabric and some glue, we'll make a new cover. The poems inside will still be the same."

Sarah gripped her sister's hand, for a moment holding it to her cheek, treasuring the closeness between them. "Thank you, Susannah," she said. "You're such a dear sister. What would I ever do without you?"

"I'm sure I don't know," Susannah said. She straightened and walked to the mirror. "Thank goodness you took my advice and got rid of that paper, Sarah. What if whoever was looking for it had found it here? It frightens me to think of what he might have done!"

She paused, and her eyes narrowed as she said, "What I don't understand is, why, after all this time, would someone have come to our room looking for that piece of paper? The logical thing would have been to come immediately after Father died."

"I have no idea," Sarah murmured, although she did know

134

the answer to Susannah's question. At first they had guessed she didn't know about Father's proof because she had not acted upon it. But now someone she had trusted had been talking—Mr. Dotson? Mr. Vonachek? Jeremy?—and the members of the syndicate were aware that she had discovered something that would be incriminating to them. Sarah looked away, knowing the guilt she felt at involving Susannah would show in her eyes. The folded papers inside her corset burned against her midriff.

"Should we tell Mrs. Hannigan about this?" Susannah asked, then answered her own question before Sarah could speak. "No, of course we can't. Father's mixed-up life, his dreadful secret—all of that is best forgotten."

With a final tug to the waistband of her skirt, Susannah opened the bedroom door. "Are you coming downstairs?" she asked.

"In a few minutes," Sarah answered. Absentmindedly she still clutched the book, but her mind churned as she tried to decide what she'd need to do next.

There was only one thing to do. Sarah quickly dropped her shoes in the wardrobe and reached for the bonnet, gloves, and scarf she'd removed.

Mr. Vonachek was the only one who had actually seen a partial copy of Father's proof, but Jeremy and Mr. Dotson were aware that she knew something about the reporter, Harry Lewis. That was enough to make them realize that if she was on Lewis's track, she must know the rest. And they knew she would have discovered these facts only if she'd found the information Father had left. It had to have been one of these three who had informed the members of the syndicate.

No. One of only *two* men—Mr. Dotson or Mr. Vonachek. It couldn't possibly be Jeremy who had told.

135

Sarah was completely aware of the danger she was now in, yet she was not afraid. A strong wave of angry determination had wiped out the fear. She was not going to allow those thieving murderers—Caulfield, Morton, and Owens—to terrify her and prevent her from uncovering the facts that would send them to jail. There was no question in her mind that they had arranged for her father's death—first through Ezekiel, and when that plan had failed, through Eli. She wouldn't wait a minute longer to seek out the mine owners.

Less than fifteen minutes later, Sarah entered the stables, which were deserted except for a bored, somewhat sleepy stable hand. She gave him instructions to saddle Lady, but as she waited for him to bring the horse, someone stepped up beside her.

"Sarah," Clint said. "I didn't know you'd be here."

Sarah whirled to face him, her heart thudding as she looked into the deep blue of his eyes. "You told me I could ride Lady at any time I wished," she said. "If you've changed your mind, I'll understand. I'll leave."

"I haven't changed my mind," he said quickly. "Lady is yours whenever you want." She could see the hurt and hope in his eyes as he asked, "Are you riding alone? Would you like company?"

As Sarah hesitated, unwilling to involve Clint in what she was planning to do, his jaw stiffened and he said, "Never mind. I shouldn't have asked." He walked a few steps away, his back to her.

Sarah was as miserable as Clint. "It's not what you think, Clint," she told him. "I'm riding alone, and it's better that way. I don't want to involve anyone else in what I'm planning to do."

Clint turned, frowning. "You're not going looking for Eli, are you?"

"No."

"Then what . . . ?"

The stable hand returned, leading Lady, who was saddled and ready to ride. Sarah couldn't tell Clint what she had discovered—not with a bystander who would hear every word.

"I'll give you a boost up," the stable hand told Sarah, and bent over, his fingers entwined to make a foothold.

As Sarah mounted, hooking her right leg over the horn on the sidesaddle, she tried to think of what she could say to Clint to ease the pain between them; but Clint was nowhere in sight.

The lump in Sarah's throat tightened, and she fought back tears. He had gone without speaking, without giving her a chance to answer.

She rode slowly from the stables, taking a northeastern route. Even though it was a Sunday afternoon, the perpetual street traffic was slow and heavy. Sarah had studied the map Mr. Vonachek had sketched and discovered that a cluster of mines on Parker's Hill was among those on the lists. Those mines would be her first destination.

Caught among slow-moving drays and carts, Sarah made little progress. She had ridden only a few blocks when a horse and rider jostled her, pushing their way to a place beside her.

"I don't care what you've got your mind set on, Sarah," Clint said. "You're not going to ride alone."

Sarah was so glad to see him that her firm resolve melted, and she smiled. "I'm glad you're here," she said.

137

He looked surprised, and the set line of his jaw relaxed. "You are?"

"I've missed you."

"Oh, Sarah . . ." Clint had to rein in his horse, who had seen an opening and darted forward. As soon as Lady came abreast of Samson, Clint blurted out, "All I've been doing is thinking about you."

The traffic began to thin, although there was a steady pattern in both directions on this road, which led to Parker's Hill. Ahead of them Sarah noticed a side road, little more than a well-trampled, dirty streak across the snow and into the pines. "Come with me," she said. "I need to talk to you."

She turned Lady, and Samson followed. When they were up above the roadway in a sheltered clearing, Sarah said, "Clint, I found the proof Father told me about." She went on to explain what he'd written and how Mr. Vonachek had uncovered the meaning of the letters.

As soon as she had finished, Clint said, "It seems to me we should hear what that Harry Lewis has to say."

"We can't. Mr. Lewis is dead." Reluctantly Sarah told Clint about her talk with Jeremy and Mr. Dotson.

She could see the flash of anger in his eyes, but he didn't refer to Jeremy. He merely asked, "Is there anything else I should know about?"

"Yes." Sarah took a deep breath and told him that someone had searched her room.

Clint scowled. "Then they know you've found that paper they were looking for. And we both know who told them."

"Be fair, Clint," Sarah said. "It could have been Mr. Vonachek. He loves a good story and isn't above being a gossip."

"You talked to him last night. When was he supposed to have found the time to tell his good story?"

"All right then, forget Mr. Vonachek," Sarah insisted. "Mr. Dotson could have gone to Chester Caulfield yesterday evening and told him what I'd asked. They'd know that if I was hunting for Harry Lewis, I would have found whatever Father had written."

"It would have been even easier for that city dude to tell his uncle."

For a moment Sarah closed her eyes and sighed. "I asked you to be fair, Clint."

"I'm being fair. There were *three* men who could have talked."

His eyes held hers, and she had to nod in agreement. "All right, but for now let's not discuss Jeremy. Please? I need to speak with as many of the mine owners as I can before the afternoon's over."

Clint shifted his holster out from under his coat, so that his Colt Peacemaker was close at hand and quick to reach. He turned Samson's head, leading the way. "Let's go," he said.

The first prospector they found was at the *Luckylou*, which apparently was living up to its name, because Lars Olson, as he introduced himself, was supervising an active crew.

His pale blond hair, leathered skin, and heavy clothing were covered with dust, but he smiled agreeably when Clint asked him if he'd answer a few questions from Sarah. "I talk some English purty good," he added, and led them down a path to the porch of his cabin.

"Mr. Olson," Sarah asked, "did Mr. Homer Morton ever come to see you about borrowing money from his bank?"

"Homer Morton? Sure." Mr. Olson smiled and swung an arm in a sweeping gesture. "I got a loan, and we doin' good. Even better."

"I know these questions are personal," Sarah asked, "but they're important, and I'm grateful to you for your answers. Did you originally have your money in Mr. Morton's bank?"

"Nope. Miners Bank, but now I'm better off with Mr. Morton's."

"Are you paying a higher interest rate?"

It took some further explanation before Mr. Olson understood, but he said, "No. Same rate."

"Did Mr. Morton take a share of your mine in order to be able to give you the loan?"

"Mr. Morton, he took nothing," Mr. Olson said.

Sarah turned to Clint. "I don't understand. How did the syndicate make this work for them?"

Mr. Olson smiled again. "I don't understand this word, *syndicate*."

"It's a group of three men," Sarah said. "We think they're benefiting from . . ." She saw that she was confusing him and searched for simpler words. "Is there anyone else besides the bank who is involved in your loan?"

He nodded. "Caumoro," he said.

"Caumoro?" Clint asked. "What does that mean?"

"The name of the people who cosigned my loan," Mr. Olson explained. "Caumoro."

"There's your syndicate," Clint told Sarah.

"Of course! Caulfield, Morton, Owens . . . It must come from the names of the three men," Sarah said, her heart beating faster with her growing excitement. "Mr. Olson, how did Caumoro become involved with your loan?"

140

"Mr. Morton tell me that Caumoro makes sure bank don't lose any money."

"What did you have to do to get Caumoro to cosign your note?" Sarah held her breath waiting for his answer.

"Only thing I do is pay them little bit each month, and I agree mine property goes to Caumoro if it fail." Mr. Olson laughed. "But I use loan to mine deeper. I find a rich, strong vein of silver, and now my mine is better than ever. It sure won't fail."

"You got a copy of the note, didn't you?" Clint asked.

"Sure. I got that. Mr. Morton tell me everything that's in it."

Sarah was puzzled. "Mr. Morton told you what was in the note? Didn't you read the note before you signed it?"

Mr. Olson laughed loudly and slapped his leg. "I can't read American language. Even I can't read Swedish. I sign with my mark, Mr. Morton gives me paper, and I have money to hire more men and dig deeper. It's good."

"Could we see the paper Mr. Morton gave you?" Sarah asked.

Mr. Olson thought a moment, then he shrugged. "Sure," he said. He disappeared into his cabin, then returned with an official envelope from the bank and handed it to Sarah.

She opened it, read through it, and said to Clint, "Caumoro owns a third of this mine and is paying itself a one-third equivalent out of the profits each month."

"No," Mr. Olson said. "That's not what Mr. Morton tell me. Caumoro is cosigner, gets paid only ten percent of the silver I bring up from my *Luckylou*."

"Mr. Morton didn't tell you the truth," Sarah said. Something else began to disturb her, and she asked, "Do you have

141

records of your own which show how much silver your mine is producing?"

"Sure," he said. "I got supervisor who knows how to read. He keeps records."

"Do you also have records from the bank which show the credit they give you for the silver you bring in?"

"Sure. They give them to me. I stick them in a box."

"Could we see them, please?"

He nodded and went to get them.

The mine's records were neatly recorded in ledger books, and it didn't take Sarah and Clint long to compare these figures with those in the bank's statements and see that the bank was consistent in not giving Mr. Olson credit for the full amount of each deposit.

"Looks like they're shorting him another ten percent," Clint said.

"Now I know what the figures next to each name on that sheet of paper mean," Sarah told him. "We'll never know how he managed to do it, but Father must have been able to see the bank's records and record the amounts of the loans."

"May I copy some of this?" she asked Mr. Olson. When he nodded agreement, she pulled some paper and a lead pencil from her purse and carefully copied figures and made notes.

As Sarah handed the papers back to Mr. Olson, she explained to him what Morton's bank was doing, but it was obvious that Mr. Olson didn't know whether to believe Sarah or not. "Maybe I ask him," he said.

"No," Sarah told him. "Don't go to Mr. Morton. Go to a lawyer. There are a number of lawyers in Leadville. One of them can help you understand your note."

Mr. Olson's face wrinkled as he tried to wrestle with the problem. Finally his features relaxed, and he shrugged. "My mine is doin' good," he said. "Got no time to go see lawyers. And got no more time for this."

As he turned to walk toward his mine, Sarah and Clint followed. Sarah was sorry that Mr. Olson was being cheated, but she could scarcely contain her excitement. She now knew the name of the syndicate and how it worked, and she was sure that when she talked to some of the other prospectors, she'd discover the same kind of crooked setup.

Chapter 14

◆　◆　◆

Three hours later, as the afternoon sun spread a thin, yellow blanket across the landscape, Sarah rode back to Leadville with Clint. "Every prospector we talked to had almost the same story," she said. "It makes me furious! Thank goodness we've got the evidence we need to put Chester Caulfield and the others in jail!"

But Clint wasn't as excited as Sarah. "You saw how most of them took the news," he said. "Their mines are doing better than ever, and they didn't want to believe you."

"They will, as soon as this scheme is made public and they find that a good share of the money they think they've got in the bank isn't there."

"Have you figured out how we're going to make this public?"

Sarah hadn't. "I—I could take this information to Marshal Kelly," she said.

"Aside from the fact that the marshal spends a lot of time in Owens' Faro Club, he's more beholdin' to Caulfield, Morton, and Owens than he is to you."

"You don't trust him?"

"Ask around. I'm not the only one who has some questions about him. Same thing goes for some of the local police."

"I don't know who to go to," Sarah said, "but it's important to make this information public."

They rode in silence a few minutes, and by the time they arrived at the outskirts of Leadville, Sarah's mind was whirling with what seemed like the only possible solution. "Jeremy could do it," she said.

Clint looked at her sharply, but before he had a chance to speak, Sarah said, "Just listen to me, Clint. Jeremy can set type and run off editions of the newspaper, and he has access to the office at night, when it's closed. He could write the story with the information we give him and expose the syndicate and its criminal activities."

"He could run to his uncle, you mean."

"Jeremy hasn't done that, and he wouldn't."

"Sarah, are you blind?"

"You're not being fair to Jeremy."

"You tell me I'm not fair? Eli Wulfe escaped shortly before we got there. I told you, the fire was still warm in the chimney, and a half-eaten meal was still on his plate. That's enough proof for me that someone tipped him off we were coming. Who else had a chance to do that?"

"It could have been someone from the marshal's office."

Clint's lips tightened, and he scowled. He dug his heels into Samson's sides, and the horse spurted forward.

Sarah tried to keep up, but Clint wove in and out among the slow-moving carts, staying just far enough ahead so that she couldn't talk to him.

By the time Sarah rode into the stables, she was angry.

146

She ignored Clint, who was busying himself with Samson, and stomped out the door. It was Sunday evening, so Jeremy would probably be at home with his aunt and uncle. Even though she'd be taking the risk of coming face-to-face with Chester Caulfield, Sarah headed in the direction of the Caulfields' house. She'd try to get the maid to call Jeremy to the door, where she could speak with him privately. Regardless of what Clint had told her, there was no other alternative.

The first part of Sarah's plan went smoothly—even better than she had anticipated. Jeremy ushered her into the parlor and told her that his aunt had retired to her room with a cup of peppermint tea and a cold compress for her headache and his uncle had gone to the Texas House for the evening with friends. When Sarah told Jeremy she had to speak to him in private, he led her to a small, cozy study and shut the door.

"Now . . . what's the mystery?" Jeremy asked as soon as Sarah had removed her coat and gloves. He slowly untied the ribbons on her bonnet and gently removed it.

"Have you come to talk about us?" he asked mischievously. He lifted one of her hands and held each fingertip to his lips.

"Jeremy, you must be serious," Sarah said, and pulled her hand away.

"I am being serious," he said.

"Please . . . sit down and listen to me," Sarah pleaded. When they were both seated, she began at the beginning, telling him what Father had told her and what she had discovered.

When she mentioned his uncle's name, Jeremy slumped back in his chair and covered his eyes with one hand. She finished her story with the visit to the prospectors, but when it was over, Jeremy didn't answer.

"I'm sorry, Jeremy," Sarah said. "Maybe I shouldn't have told you about your uncle."

"Maybe you shouldn't," he said. He sat up, leaning forward in his chair so that their shoulders were almost touching. There was no sparkle of fun in Jeremy's face now. His expression was so solemn that Sarah became frightened. She stayed where she was without moving, but she wondered if he could hear the thumping of her heart.

Mustering all her courage, Sarah said, "I hoped you would help me make this information public through *The Star*."

"You want me to use my uncle's own newspaper to discredit him and bring his arrest?"

Sarah flushed. "I'm sorry. I was asking too much."

She moved to rise, but Jeremy gripped her arms so firmly, she couldn't move. "Everything was fine, Sarah," he said. "In spite of myself, I enjoyed my newspaper job, and I like living in comfort with my uncle and aunt. Now, because of you, it's over."

Sarah gulped, unable to speak, as fear tightened her throat.

After a long pause Jeremy said, "Maybe I was growing too content, too complacent. Maybe it's time for me to move on. Remember, I told you that in the spring I wanted to travel to California, or Oregon . . . with you."

Sarah caught her breath. "I—I don't understand what you're telling me."

Now it was Jeremy's turn to look puzzled. "Why don't you? You knew that no matter what you asked, I'd help you, didn't you? Isn't that why you came?"

"Yes," Sarah answered. "Of course it is."

"I'm not doing this only for you, Sarah," Jeremy said. "Truth can't be hidden. It must be told. I'd be as guilty as Uncle Chester if I didn't print this. So during the night I'll write the story, set the type, and run off a special edition of *The Star*. I'll see that it gets distributed early tomorrow morning." He straightened his shoulders, and a businesslike tone came into his voice as he said, "Give me the proof you've collected."

"I've got it right here." Sarah handed him the notes she had made at the mines.

Jeremy glanced through them and began asking questions. For quite a while Sarah added details and gave Jeremy the full names of each prospector she had visited.

"It would help if I could look over a few of the bank records," Jeremy told her, "but we've got enough information here to make an accurate story, and the bank's records can be seized later by the courts."

Sarah waited patiently while Jeremy carefully went through the notes again. Finally he asked, "Where's the information your father left you?"

"I can give you a copy."

"A copy's not proof. I need the original in Ben Lindley's own handwriting."

"If this case goes to trial, we'll need it."

Jeremy nodded. "I know, but you'll have to trust me, Sarah. I'll take care of it."

She no longer hesitated. "I have it . . . on my person. If you'll give me a few moments of privacy, I'll be able to give it to you."

And a very short time later she did. As Jeremy took the paper, studying it intently, Sarah stretched to kiss him on the cheek. "Thank you, Jeremy," she said.

149

He didn't try to kiss her in return. He didn't even smile. This was a Jeremy she didn't know. Had she made a mistake in trusting him?

It was too late to wonder or worry. All Sarah could do was count on Jeremy not to fail her.

Chapter 15

•   •   •

Jeremy escorted Sarah home, reluctantly leaving her at Mrs. Hannigan's porch. "When all this is over, we'll have important things to talk about," he said. He strode down the street in the direction of the newspaper office.

Jeremy was sacrificing everything in order to do as Sarah had asked, and she owed him more than she could ever repay. She had given him her friendship, but maybe friendship wasn't enough. Jeremy might ask for more in return.

Sarah should have been thrilled that she was fulfilling her promise to her father, that during tomorrow's morning hours the entire town of Leadville would learn about the crimes of three of its leading citizens. When these men were no longer a threat, witnesses would come forward; it would soon come out that her father had shot only in self-defense, and his name would be cleared. However, there was a quiet sadness within Sarah, an emptiness she couldn't understand.

Many of the boarders had retired in preparation for the first day of a work week, which meant an early rising. Sarah had missed supper, but that didn't matter. She wasn't hungry.

The fire in the fireplace had been banked, and only one lamp had been left burning in the parlor, its wick sputtering as it flickered dimly, shooting long shadows that slid across the room and into the darkness at the top of the stairs. Sarah stopped to pick it up and peered into the hallway, where she thought she'd seen movement. "Is anyone else down here?" she called softly.

Mrs. Hannigan suddenly came out of the downstairs hallway, flustered and nervously smoothing down the skirt of her dress. "This is no time for a proper young lady to be coming home!" she said. Prepared for a scolding, Sarah wondered why Mrs. Hannigan didn't ask her where she had been. Instead the landlady tempered her words with a quick hug and said, "Get up to bed now. You have to rise early tomorrow morning."

She took Sarah's arm, and at the top of the stairs, with a whispered "good night," Mrs. Hannigan slipped into her bedroom. A few minutes later Sarah was surprised to find that the girls' room was empty. What was Susannah doing downstairs at this hour?

Unwilling to pass Mrs. Hannigan's bedroom, in case the woman would hear the creak of the floorboards in the hall, Sarah tiptoed as quietly as she could toward the back stairway. She emerged into the pantry and entered the kitchen to find Susannah still working, scouring the iron plates on top of the stove.

Susannah's eyes opened wide when she saw Sarah. "Where were you?" she demanded. "You didn't tell me. No one knew."

"I was with Jeremy," Sarah said, avoiding a direct answer.

152

As far as Susannah knew, the words Father had written had been destroyed. *Tomorrow, when the newspaper is out, and it's all over,* she promised herself, *I'll tell Susannah everything.* "You were with Jeremy all this time?" Susannah looked pleased.

"It's late," Sarah said. "Why in the world are you still up? And cleaning the stove, at that?"

"I was waiting for you, and because I was worried, it helped to stay busy."

Sarah moved toward the dining-room door, but Susannah ran ahead of her and closed the door. "We need to talk, Sarah," she said, "and if any of the boarders are still downstairs, I don't want them to hear us."

"No one else is downstairs, and anyone who might go to the parlor would never be able to hear us, even with the door open." Sarah was wary.

But Susannah's tone became conversational, and she smiled. "I had the most interesting conversation with Mr. Vonachek about our boardinghouse," she said. "He told me that he'd explained things to you, and I must say that his idea makes sense. I can't abide just handing over that fine piece of property to Uncle Amos and Aunt Cora."

She chattered on. "My goodness, Sarah, in three months you'll be eighteen, and you know that by the time a woman reaches nineteen, her chances for making a good marriage are lessened considerably."

"Hush, Susannah! Please!" Sarah put a finger to her sister's lips. "I don't want to talk about our boardinghouse right now. I'm so tired that all I want to do is sleep. I've got a class to teach tomorrow."

Susannah studied her a moment and sighed. "I keep forgetting that you're a teacher. Things are so different for us

153

now, aren't they? Remember that only a short while ago you were so frightened you nearly fainted when you thought about traveling to the West to find Father? And now you seem to be at home here."

"Yes," Sarah said. "I remember." The mirror reflected what looked like the same Sarah, but it couldn't show the determination that made her feel stronger, or the confidence that helped her make decisions and stand by them.

She held out a hand to Susannah. "Time for bed," she said. She walked toward the table on which she'd placed her purse and the oil lamp.

Behind her the back door to the kitchen creaked open softly, and a voice said, "Don't make no noise, ladies, or one of you is goin' to get hurt."

Susannah gasped loudly as they both whirled to face the man who stood there.

"Eli Wulfe!" Sarah cried, immediately recognizing the dark wildness in his eyes.

Wulfe's left hand shot out. He clamped it down on Susannah's shoulder, jerking her toward him as he gestured with the gun in his right hand. "I told you," he said in a low voice, "any noise and one of you would get hurt. Well, it's gonna be this one."

"No, don't!" Sarah said, forcing her voice to little over a whisper. "Please don't hurt her. We'll do as you ask."

"That makes it easy," he said. "Hand over whatever it was you got from your father."

"We don't have it!" Susannah insisted. "Sarah burnt it!"

He stared so hard at Sarah that she couldn't meet his eyes. "You're lyin'," he said to Susannah.

Sarah took a deep breath and tried to stay calm. "I don't have it!" she said. "That is the truth."

154

"But you know where it is," he countered. "And I been sent to get it."

"Please leave us alone," Sarah begged. "I don't have the paper, and I can't give it to you."

"I'll give you a chance to think it over," Eli said. He shoved Susannah roughly, and she stumbled, nearly falling. "Put your coat on," he ordered.

"It's upstairs."

He waved the gun in Sarah's direction. "Then give her yours. Hurry."

"What are you doing?" Sarah asked.

"I'm taking your sister with me, with or without a coat, and it's mighty cold outside."

While her mind wrestled with a way to stop Eli from carrying out his plan, Sarah followed his instructions.

"Sarah, I don't want to go with him!" Susannah whimpered, but with a muttered threat Eli whipped the coat around her, and she obediently shoved her arms into the sleeves and buttoned it.

"You ain't got a choice," Eli said. He glared at Sarah. "If you want her back tomorrow morning, bring that paper to the schoolhouse. We'll make a trade."

"You can't do this!" Sarah cried.

But Eli growled, "It wouldn't worry me none to take care of her like I took care of your father. Think about that."

"Oh, Sarah!" Susannah wept. "Help me!"

In desperation Sarah lunged for her purse and the derringer she kept inside it, but Eli was too fast for her. With a backward swipe of his left hand, he knocked her against the wall. She bounced off, banging her head so hard that she couldn't see, and fell to the floor.

Her ears buzzed with noises and shadows that tried to drag

155

her into a black pit, and she fought against them, aware that somewhere there was help and she would have to find it. She would go to Jeremy and beg him not to print that special edition. . . . It was the only way to save Susannah. She tried to get to her feet but dropped to the floor again as a steadier thought wiped out her panic. Jeremy himself had said that the truth must be told, that if he didn't print the story, he'd be no better than his uncle. *And if I stopped him,* Sarah thought, *I'd be every bit as guilty as those men in the Caumoro.* Nobody would blame her for stopping the story to save her sister, but maybe there was a way to save Susannah *and* see the story in print. There had to be something she could do.

There *was* something. She'd find Clint. "Clint?" she cried aloud. She managed to get to her hands and knees. "Clint. Where are you?"

"I'm here, Sarah," she heard him say, and she felt herself lifted to her feet and held tightly.

While her head gradually cleared, she became aware that Clint wasn't a hallucination. The slightly salty smell of his skin, his breath warm against her cheek . . . He was actually there with her. And someone else was in the room—Mr. Vonachek, his long, heavy coat draped over the nightshirt that ended at his knees.

Sarah glanced at his bare, hairy legs. What would normally have been a shocking breach of privacy didn't seem to matter at all.

"My room is above the kitchen," Mr. Vonachek told Clint. "I heard someone fall. Was it Miss Lindley? What happened to her?"

Fully conscious, Sarah pulled away from Clint and pressed a hand to her throbbing head. "Eli Wulfe was here! He took

156

Susannah!" she cried. "I tried to stop him, but he struck me." She grabbed Clint's arms. "Help me, Clint! We have to follow them!"

"Did he give any idea of where he was taking her?" Clint asked.

Sarah stopped, her mouth open. "No." There was something that should give her the answer, but what was it? If only her head would stop hurting!

Mr. Vonachek broke in. "What was the purpose of the abduction? Was it revenge because you shot him?"

"No," Sarah answered. "He told me I had to give him the paper Father wrote."

"The paper?" Mr. Vonachek whistled in surprise. "This has to do with the code I solved for you, doesn't it?"

"Yes. Chester Caulfield, Homer Morton, and Wilbur Owens formed a syndicate. They're cheating some of the prospectors. Jeremy has the information. He'll show it to you. He's printing a special edition of *The Star* to distribute in the morning."

Clint grunted in disbelief, but Mr. Vonachek said, "Eli Wulfe is working for Chester Caulfield? Well! Then it wasn't just circumstance that led him to hide out in Caulfield's abandoned shack."

Sarah's mouth fell open. "Clint!" she cried. "That's it! *The Sweet Violet* mine in Bartlett Gulch! Caulfield's other cabin! It's where he's taken Susannah!"

"Get your coat," Clint told her. "It won't take us long to get there."

Helplessly Sarah said, "He took my coat."

Mr. Vonachek took off his own coat and held it out to Sarah. "I have another one upstairs," he said. "I'll get dressed and roust out some of the members of the Merchants

157

Protective Patrol. It's not just Eli Wulfe who should be taken into custody."

Sarah flinched at his suggestion. "There can't be any more lynchings," she pleaded.

"I firmly agree," Mr. Vonachek said solemnly, and a wave of pain momentarily darkened his face. "The hangings were born of desperation, but afterwards, as we saw the bodies swinging in the night breeze, some of us were sickened at what we had done." He paused while he struggled to get his emotions under control, then said, "We will take these men into custody, and turn them over to the marshal and make sure the law is enforced."

"Thank you," Sarah said. She pulled on Mr. Vonachek's coat and the gloves she found stuffed into one pocket and ran out the back door after Clint.

"We won't take time to get Lady saddled," Clint told Sarah. He untied Samson's lead, then leapt into the saddle, holding out a hand. "Climb up behind me," he said as he swung her upward, "and hold tight."

Sarah did as he said, resting her head against his shoulders. As they made their way as fast as possible through the crowded streets, she asked, "How did you happen to be at Mrs. Hannigan's?"

"I told her you might be in danger and I wanted to be on hand to protect you," he said. "I followed you ever since you went off in a huff at the stables. When you and that reporter set off for Mrs. Hannigan's, I went on ahead and got her permission to spend the night sitting at the bottom of her front stairs."

"Oh, Clint," Sarah said. "Then you already knew I'd taken the notes to Jeremy."

"I figured as much."

"He's going to make up a special edition. He's going to write about exactly what happened, even though his uncle was a part of the crime."

"So you said. Do you believe that?"

"Of course I do! We went over all the notes I'd made, and he asked dozens of questions. That's what took so long."

"You didn't give him the paper your father left, did you?"

"Well, yes," Sarah answered, her face even warmer. "Jeremy said he had to have it, so I did."

Clint muttered something under his breath, and Sarah could feel his muscles tense.

They had left the town behind, and Clint picked up the pace. Sarah didn't try to talk, so they rode in silence.

When they reached the cabin, Clint pulled in Samson and helped Sarah slide from the horse. He jumped down and tethered Samson out of the way, inside a nearby cluster of aspens, whose bare white limbs shone like skeletons in the moonlight. Narrow slivers of light squeezed from between the cracks in the walls, and from behind the shack a horse nervously whinnied.

Samson whinnied in return.

"Damn!" Clint said. "Wulfe'll know someone's here."

"Then we'll have to act fast," Sarah said. "Why don't I go to the door and call out that I've brought the paper he wants? When he opens the door, we'll push our way in."

A curtain that covered a window next to the door was pulled back just enough for someone to peer through.

Clint melted back into the trees and removed his Peacemaker from its holster. "Remember that Wulfe will be armed. I'm sure he won't have it in mind to harm *you* . . . at least until he gets that paper he wants, so I think it's safe enough for you to go to the door. Try to keep from going inside, and if I yell for you to drop, do it and don't stop to ask questions."

"You'll be with me, won't you?"

"I'll be on hand. . . . Go on now. He'll get suspicious if you wait too long."

Sarah walked ahead, noticing the window curtain drop back into place, and as she neared the shack, she called out, "Eli Wulfe, it's me! Sarah Lindley!"

"What are you doin' here?" he yelled through the closed door.

"I brought the paper with the information Father wrote on it. And I want you to release my sister."

The door opened a crack, and Sarah could see the shine of the gun barrel in Wulfe's hand. "Are you alone?"

"Yes," Sarah answered. "I'm alone."

With one swift movement the door opened, and Sarah found herself jerked inside. Then the door banged shut, and a stout wooden bar dropped across it.

This wasn't the plan. Clint had told her to try to keep from going inside the cabin. Sarah could hear her heart throbbing in her ears as Wulfe stared at her with reddened, bloodshot eyes. Now what was she going to do?

With all her strength Sarah willed herself to stand straight and tall and have the courage to look past him to where Susannah sat on the edge of a cot. Her wrists were bound together, and she was crying.

"Well? Where's the paper?" Wulfe demanded.

Sarah scowled at him so fiercely that he stumbled back a step. "You wait!" she ordered. "I'll get to you later!" She turned and ripped the gag off of her sister's mouth.

"Susannah, tell me . . . has he hurt you?" She held her breath, afraid to hear the answer.

"Of course he hurt me!" Susannah exploded. "He tied my wrists with that rough cord, and he slapped me, and even threw me in the door." She raised both hands to point at the swollen, discolored bruise at the left side of her face. As Susannah went on indignantly about Eli Wulfe smelling like a pigsty and growling terrible threats at her, Sarah took a long, shuddering breath of relief.

"Untie my sister," Sarah ordered Wulfe.

"Not till I get that paper," he insisted.

Even though Wulfe probably couldn't read, and wouldn't know one written note from another, Sarah had no paper at all to give him. As he slowly turned the gun toward Susannah, Sarah began to panic. Where was Clint?

"Don't let him shoot me!" Susannah screamed.

At that moment one of the windows exploded as Clint leapt through. A blast of gunshot shook the room, and Sarah heard the crack of splintered bone in Wulfe's right arm.

With a wild squeal of pain, he dropped his gun, and Sarah scooped it up.

Eli Wulfe fell into a chair, moaning and crying, and Sarah glanced around the room looking for something with which to help him. She grabbed her scarf, which Susannah had worn and bound it tightly around Wulfe's arm to staunch the bleeding; then she tied his arm across his chest for support.

While Clint secured Wulfe's left wrist to the back of his belt, Sarah unfastened the cord around Susannah's wrists.

"Susannah, I'm so sorry this happened to you!" Sarah

cried, and reached for her sister, but Susannah dashed to Clint, flinging her arms around his neck and sobbing against his chest.

As Clint bent to hold Susannah, clumsily patting her shoulder, Sarah turned away, sick at heart. It was her fault that Susannah had been put through such a horrifying, frightening ordeal. And it was her fault that she and Clint had quarreled. If Susannah and Clint . . .

But Clint took Susannah by the shoulders and turned her to face Sarah. "Here, Sarah," he said uncomfortably. "Your sister needs you."

As Sarah gathered Susannah into her arms, Clint raised the bar that lay across the door. "I'll go out and saddle Wulfe's horses," he said, and closed the door behind him.

Susannah looked up at Sarah with swollen eyes and said, "Clint doesn't love me, and he never will. He loves *you,* Sarah."

Desperately, unsuccessfully, Sarah tried to think of the right thing to say, but Susannah pulled away, tossed back her head, and went on. "Maybe I don't even care! Well, not much."

"Susannah, dear," Sarah began.

"Don't 'Susannah dear' me! And stop treating me as though I were a *child!*"

"I'll never do it again!" Sarah promised, as she flung her arms about Susannah and hugged her tightly. "You've been brave and wonderful, and I'm proud of you."

For a moment they clung together, ignoring Wulfe's mumbled cursing and moaning.

"You were right about at least one thing, Sarah," Susannah said. She walked away, smoothing her hair and tugging down the skirt of her oversized coat. "I'm really not ready to get married. If I can't have . . . that is, I want time to make other plans, so I'd like to stay on with Mrs. Hannigan for a while, and then go back to Chicago. I told you about Mr. Vonachek's plans for our boardinghouse, didn't I?" She interrupted herself to say, "Do you realize that Mr. Vonachek is really a highly intelligent, very successful businessman?"

Chapter 16

◆   ◆   ◆

Jeremy was drooping with exhaustion and had dark circles under his eyes when he brought Sarah a copy of the special edition of *The Leadville Daily Star* the next morning. He also placed in her hand the sheet of paper on which her father had written the incriminating information.

Sarah busied her students with seat work so that she could glance over the front page of *The Star,* and as she read, she praised Jeremy for his story.

"Some members of the Merchants Protective Patrol came for Uncle Chester last night," Jeremy told her. "Homer Morton's in custody, too, but they're still looking for Wilbur Owens."

"Mr. Vonachek promised they'd be given a fair trial," Sarah assured him.

He nodded. "They also told Uncle they'd go through the legal system to see that the people who'd been cheated would get their money returned to them. Uncle blustered and threatened when they took him off to jail, but it didn't do any good, because I heard from Deputy Spradley that Eli

165

Wulfe had told everyone within hearing how he and his brother were hired to commit the murders." He pointed to the lower right-hand section of the page. "The part about your father is in the story in the last column."

"Thank you," Sarah murmured. She was filled with a lightness, a joyfulness, a wonderful sense of freedom. She had accomplished what seemed to be an impossible task. She had kept her promise to her father. Benjamin Lindley's name had been cleared.

But it hadn't been only her father who had been hurt. She looked at Jeremy with concern as she asked, "What's going to happen to your aunt?"

"Aunt Violet is going to sell the newspaper. *The Carbonate Chronicle* has made some offers for it in the past, so she's fairly sure they'll still want it. When that's taken care of, Aunt Violet is going to Denver to live with her brother." He shrugged. "It's surprising, but she seems to have perked up. I think she's going to appreciate her new life. Uncle Chester bullies her."

"I'm sorry that it was *your* uncle who was involved," Sarah murmured.

Jeremy tried a smile. "Well, turnabout's fair play. You escaped from your uncle. Now, I'll escape from mine."

Sarah looked up sharply. "Escape? But you told me you were happy."

"I also told you I was getting complacent. If I'd stayed on in Leadville, I might have been happy here forever. But I want to write novels! I plan to explore new worlds!"

Jeremy glanced quickly at the students, who—all but Mercy Klinger—pretended they weren't listening and immediately bent over their work. Lowering his voice, he said,

"Sarah, you're ready for a new life, too. Will you come with me and share mine?"

Sarah saw the longing and hope in his eyes. "Jeremy," she whispered, "you're my very dear friend, but I can't . . ."

"Friend? Please . . . don't say it." In order to stop her words, he put his fingertips against her lips.

Mercy giggled, and a few heads bobbed up, the children staring.

Mindful of the audience Jeremy took a step closer and quietly said, "It hurts to be told I'm only a dear friend, when I want to be so much more to you."

"You *do* mean a great deal to me. I owe you so much."

Jeremy moaned and said, "Sarah, how can you say that when I handed information to my uncle which he used to harm you?"

"It wasn't your fault."

"During the moments I feel the most guilty—such as now—forgiveness is harder to take than blame."

"Oh, Jeremy," Sarah asked, "what do you want me to say?"

"I want you to tell me you love me," he whispered.

"I do—but not as a—a wife would love you. Please understand, Jeremy, I don't want to hurt you," Sarah insisted, her eyes blurring with tears.

Jeremy stepped back and tried to assume a nonchalant pose. "It probably wouldn't have worked anyway," he whispered. "You and I are too much alike. We're both dreamers and—"

"I am not just a dreamer!" Sarah interrupted.

"Don't deny it. Be glad you're a dreamer," he told her. "Deep inside your beautiful mind, Sarah, is a spark that will never go out unless you let it."

167

Sarah smiled. "I said I'm not *just* a dreamer, Jeremy. I've begun to realize that while I'm very much like my father in some ways, I also have some very different qualities. I'm my own person. I've found that I can take charge of my own life and make my own choices."

His voice dropped again, and she could hear the pain behind it as he said, "Like choosing Clint."

"Oh, Jeremy," she murmured, "I didn't mean to hurt you."

"Don't worry about me," he told her. "I'll get over it." He took her hands and held them tightly. "Promise me that you'll always follow your dreams, and I'll promise you that someday I'll write a novel about a very special woman named Sarah."

He left the schoolroom, with the gaze of the children riveted to him in fascination, and Sarah knew that there'd be many embellished answers that evening when mothers asked, "Tell me what happened in school today."

That afternoon, as she stood on the steps dismissing her students, Clint arrived. He waited patiently until every child had left, then followed Sarah inside the classroom. "I came to eat crow," he told her, and gestured toward the extra edition of *The Leadville Daily Star* that still lay on her desk. "You were right about him, and I was wrong. He did what you asked, which took a lot of courage."

Sarah stood before Clint, looking into his incredible eyes, and wishing she could reach up and entwine her fingers in his short, thick, black curls. Clint had never looked so handsome, so totally and completely wonderful.

"I hope you know it took courage for me to come here and say this to you," he mumbled.

"I know," she said.

168

"I need to get something straight between us, Sarah, before I go on and say what else is in my mind. I can't give you the kind of life that—that newspaperman can give you. For a while, until I make a success of the ranch, I won't be able to give you much at all, yet I'd be asking an awful lot from you."

"What are you saying, Clint?" Sarah asked. "Are you proposing marriage?"

"I don't know what I'm saying." Clint groaned. "All I know is that I love you, Sarah, and I can't stand thinking that you might turn me down."

"I wouldn't turn you down," Sarah said. "I love you, too. I don't care about possessions, and I'm not afraid of hard work. I *want* to be a part of your dream, because you're a part of mine, and . . ."

Sarah couldn't finish because Clint's mouth was on hers, and she eagerly returned the kiss. As he held her, Sarah reached up and tangled her fingers in Clint's thick, curly hair.

About the Author

JOAN LOWERY NIXON is the acclaimed author of more than eighty fiction and nonfiction books for children and young adults. She is a three-time winner of the Mystery Writers of America Edgar Award and the recipient of many Children's Choice Awards. Her popular books for young adults include *High Trail to Danger*, the bestselling Orphan Train Quartet, for which she received two Golden Spur Awards, and the Hollywood Daughters trilogy.

Mrs. Nixon and her husband live in Houston, Texas.